ANGEL HUNTS
SOUL FORGE BOOK ONE

LESLIE CLAIRE WALKER

My name is Night Sanchez.
Every choice I make is a second chance.

The Order raised me to be a true believer and a killer—until I met the gaze of an unusual girl marked for death. Saving that girl and raising her can't wash the blood from my hands. But nothing matters more than protecting her.

So when the Order I betrayed tracks us down, I'm ready for the fight. But it's not just the Order that wants my kid. The Angel of Death wants her, too. Suddenly, this is so much bigger than us.

I can't fight the forces of Heaven and Hell on my own. Trust comes hard, but I have to lean on those who could become family if I let them get close. Can they handle my secrets?

The tougher question is, can I? A cage within my mind hides the worst of them—and the most powerful magic. I have to be brave enough to break those walls, or the Order and the Angel win. My girl —and what remains of my soul—will be lost.

Explore the first book of the complete Soul Forge series. Meet the daring people who fight for love, life, hope—and each other.

ALSO BY LESLIE CLAIRE WALKER

THE AWAKENED MAGIC SAGA

THE SOUL FORGE

(The Complete Series)

Angel Hunts

Angel Rises

Angel Falls

Angel Strikes

Angel Roars

Angel Burns

THE FAERY CHRONICLES

(The Complete Series)

Faery Novice

Faery Prophet

Faery Sovereign

SHORT STORY COLLECTIONS

Ink & Blood

Ink & Stars

Ink & Sword

*This book is dedicated to Kristine Kathryn Rusch,
without whom it may never have been written.
Thank you for that workshop assignment,
for the opportunity to learn so much from you,
and for your wonderful friendship.*

CHAPTER 1

PORTLAND, OREGON, stretched and yawned, awakening around me in the hour before dawn. I shivered as the November chill bit through the black fleece of my hoodie, and a wicked wind gusted from the west, spiraling the fine drops of mist in the air. The traffic light at the corner flipped from red to green, the hum of engines and the slick of tires on wet concrete a comfort to my wired nerves.

I stood beneath the dripping overhang in front of Justice Gym, go-cup of black coffee in hand. I listened and scanned the neighborhood for anything out of the ordinary. My life depended on it.

Twenty yards to the right, around the corner at the neighborhood stop-n-shop on Burnside, a car door slammed. Sleepy voices wafted my way. People stopping for smokes or snacks. Harmless.

To my left, the street curved and forked, parallel-parked cars huddled inches apart for warmth at the curbs. Out of the dark, the Orange Warrior materialized in his neon-orange rain suit, bike tires splashing through the puddled light of the street lamps. He caught sight of me and flashed the peace sign and called out, "Hey! Morning!"

I gave him a thumbs-up. Then he whizzed past on his way to work, the headlamp on the front of his helmet beaming like a search light, the red light on the back of his bike blinking fast enough to give somebody a seizure.

The golden halo around his body—the manifestation of the life force that moved through him—lit him up like a firework to my magical sight.

Across the street, the Stump Town Diner spoke the language of my belly, the rich aromas of dark-roasted coffee, salty, crisp bacon, and fresh-baked bread streaming from inside each time the door opened. Blond Bagel Girl, wrapped in her hooded purple raincoat, slipped inside for her usual breakfast to go. She shone with the same gold as the cyclist, though more muted, melancholy.

It was beautiful. Normal.

Normals in my neighborhood, going about their normal lives like clockwork. I'd never be one of them. I'd look over my shoulder until the day I died.

I turned the key in the lock of the gym door, same as every other day for the last three months since I'd moved to town. That my boss, Red Jennings, trusted a woman so secretive and new to the city with his life's work said a lot about him. A woman without much money and a teenage kid in tow, no less. Most people would call him a fool, but I chose to believe he was an uncommonly good judge of character. One who backed up his judgment with thorough background checks.

He hadn't batted an eye when I'd asked to be paid in cash, though; my existence kept off his books. When he asked the occasional personal question, I talked around it rather than answering directly, and he didn't give me any crap about it. He'd run a check on me and found it unremarkable. Of course, it was an unremarkable lie that I'd built through illegal channels and paid for with blood money, but all Red knew was that I wasn't a criminal, that he and I shared a hometown in Houston, Texas, and we shared a soft spot for troubled kids.

I pushed my way into the narrow front room of the gym, the electronic bell above the door chiming. I flipped the light switches with the flat of one hand and inhaled the perfume of rubber, bleach wipes, and sweat as the overhead fluorescents buzzed to life. The lights threw the entry into sharp relief: the interlocked, black rubber mats that covered the concrete floor, the triple-stacked row of black plastic cubbies and lockers that covered the long wall in front of me, and the donated, brown suede sofa on the right, its seats so deep I sometimes wondered whether it ate people as well as car keys and loose change. I keyed the code into the alarm, hung a right and then a left, bouncing down the short staircase onto the gym floor.

It shared the dimension of a good-sized basketball court. The walls had been painted white once upon a time, but had been scuffed and scratched to head-height. All the essential equipment hugged the walls: long barbells pegged into metal stands, kettlebells, weight racks, and benches for presses. Pull-up bars, medicine balls, wooden boxes for jumping. The back wall of the gym consisted of garage doors that could be opened in the summer for air flow. Two climbing ropes hung suspended from the ceiling. Also in back, a dozen rowing machines stood on end beside the water fountain, bathrooms, and small table that held the sound system.

It felt like home. First one I'd ever truly had. I had chosen it, and it had chosen me.

The first class started in thirty minutes, at 6:00 a.m. The usual suspects would file in: kids whose parents dropped them here before school trying to buy peace of mind—a little activity to help keep their progeny calm, quiet, and cooperative during a long day of sitting, obedience, and memorization. The usual suspects were anything but normal.

They didn't seem to belong anywhere, or to anyone except each other. They had halos that spoke of magic, all of it benign. They'd adopted my kid into their group as soon as they laid eyes on her, for which I felt profoundly grateful. Like Red had with me, they trusted her right away, even knowing nothing about her. For instance, the fact that she wasn't my daughter. She was no relation at all.

The first time I'd seen her, she'd been ten, close to the age I'd been when magic had marked me. I'd broken in to her house with orders to kill her family. To kill her. I hadn't been able to do it.

Faith Torres, her name had been then, before we'd gone into

hiding with new identities, new lives, and nightmares that plagued our dreams. Ten years old then, now fifteen. Now she was Faith Sanchez, with dark chocolate hair that swung to the middle of her back, gangly arms and legs she hadn't quite grown into yet, and a hard-to-say-no-to million-watt smile. She also had a big, geeky love for badass super-heroines and a growing rebellious streak.

She'd sneaked out last night. First time ever, sometime between midnight and 2:00 a.m. When I'd made my nightly security round at 3:30, glass of tap water in hand, I found pillows under the down comforter and a window open just a crack, sucking in the cold. The water I'd downed on the way into the room flash-froze inside my belly at the sight.

I fought to shake ice-cold panic that told me the people we'd run from had located us and taken Faith, that there was no safe place and would never be, that the death I'd saved Faith from waited for her just around the corner, or maybe had already been dealt.

The Order of the Blood Moon's magical assassins were relentless. No one left the Order. They didn't forgive, and they didn't forget.

I shook off the panic. I calmed myself like the pro I'd been. Like the pro I still could be.

The Order had taken me in during a time I'd been desperate and vulnerable. They'd stripped me of my name, my identity, and the last shards of my childhood innocence. They helped me to marshal my magic, training me to gather information, conceal myself, kill, and elude capture. I'd given them my heart and soul because I'd had no one and nothing else to give it to. I'd allowed them to turn me into a stone cold killer. I'd done more than that—I'd embraced it. Our association had lasted fifteen years, until two months after my twenty-seventh birthday, the night I met Faith.

Looking at her empty bed, breathing through my fear, I let my training take over. I searched for a sign someone had taken her, but found no trace of foul play. After that, I'd pinged the GPS on her cell and located her at Ben's house. He was one of her new friends. His single father traveled on business too much and left him home alone.

Ben, who would never hurt Faith.

Still, I hadn't slept a wink the rest of the night. My girl hadn't climbed back through the window before time for me to head out for work—and I'd had no choice but to leave—so I'd put a note on her pillow. When she came home, she'd get the message and get her ass to the gym before school to explain herself. She'd show, too. No avoiding me, because that would be dumb. No one could ever accuse her of stupidity.

I made my way toward the back of the gym, setting down my go-cup on the shelf beside the sound system, then striking up my favorite classic rock playlist. I shrugged out of my hoodie and ran my fingers through my long, black hair, tying it up into a ponytail. I could fit in a warm-up and a few rope climbs myself while I waited for the door to open, getting myself in order before working the same movement with the kids. It'd take my mind off waiting for Faith as well.

The electronic bell over the front door chimed. I turned toward the whisper of denim and the squelch of wet shoes on rubber, expecting to find Faith walking in, a cranky apology on her lips and a sheepish expression on her face.

No.

Time slowed. I blinked, the movement seeming to take minutes rather than seconds. The air felt thick—almost too thick to breathe.

Before I even laid eyes on my visitor, the cadence of the walk struck me wrong, the footsteps belonging to someone heavier and with finer motor control of their body than my fifteen-year-old. I breathed in deep and tasted a hint of amber and vanilla in the air. None of the moms or stepmoms or girlfriends I'd met wore that scent. I'd studied each of them, remembered every quirky detail. I knew them. I couldn't afford not to.

I knew my visitor, too. I'd just never counted on seeing her again, because I'd never counted on seeing any of my colleagues from the Order again. Especially not this one.

The woman who'd walked through the door stopped ten feet from me, a signal she intended to talk rather than attack. Really, it was unnecessary. If she'd meant to harm me, I'd never have seen or heard her coming.

She pushed back the hood of her black rain slicker. Her blond curls had grown all the way to her shoulders since the last time I'd run my fingers through them. The only makeup she wore on her porcelain face was a pale pink flush of lipstick; her dark blue eyes were sharp on me. She unzipped her jacket, letting it fall open. A black brocade vest accented her long-sleeved black T-shirt. The ensemble hugged the curves of her breasts, skimming the line of her waist. Water soaked the hems of her black jeans. She wore steel-toe black boots with rubber soles.

Sunday Sloan. Once upon a time, my salvation.

The halo around her body held a tint of rose red, life force flavored with a strong, blinding passion that she harnessed in everything she did, including her kills. One look in the eyes of her victims, and she could literally blind them if she chose. She had a touch of the traditional psychic as well, not enough to actually see the future, but enough to guess what might happen that would affect her most and allow her to act accordingly.

The same magical gifts infiltrated her personal relationships. Her faults became hard to see. And once she made up her mind about a cause or a person, she gave them her unconditional, undying—blind—loyalty. I'd been on the receiving end of that loyalty. I'd thrown it away when I'd left without saying goodbye.

Sunday Sloan was the Order's MVP. Or MVO—most valuable operative.

If she was here, I was in deep trouble. I'd missed something important. Had I been wrong last night—had Sunday or someone who traveled with her taken Faith? Had they used their talents to make me believe Faith was safe at Ben's? Was Faith already dead?

How had Sunday found me? My passive magic—reading halos—couldn't be tracked by anyone. My active magic, on the other hand—using my power to influence others—could be. I'd been careful. I'd only used that active power on myself since I'd left the Order. It was the best way to unlock the secrets hidden in my own mind. And to stay sharp in case a day like this ever dawned.

I cleared my throat. "I didn't hide well enough?"

Sunday's voice had a liquid quality to it, like water flowing over river rocks. "You did. It's just that I know you better than the ones who're hunting you."

She'd just implied she wasn't hunting me, but that others were. If the Order had sent someone, Sunday would be it.

"I'm out, Night," she said. "Just like you."

She called me by my new alias rather than the name the Order had given me. It felt disorienting to hear it roll off her tongue.

"How did you get out?" I asked.

"I killed the Ghost," she said.

The Ghost. Brown hair, middling height, average weight. No distinguishing physical characteristics. He could pass you on the street and your eyes would skip over him. It wouldn't fool experienced bodyguards for more than a few minutes, but by the time they saw him, they'd be dead.

His mentor had named him appropriately.

He'd been our friend. One of the few people inside the Order I'd let in.

"He threaten you?" I asked.

"No," she said. "But he was in the way. He could tell something was off with me. He wouldn't let it go."

I closed my eyes for a second. A bit of my old life flashed forward from memory: lying in the fine, white sand of a Mexican beach with this woman before she'd been my lover, listening to the rhythm of the waves crashing, one after the other, on the shore, watching the cloudless blue sky with a clear conscience. The memory felt a thousand years old.

The Ghost had traveled with us on that trip, teasing us about our chemistry together. Sunday had killed him. She'd killed to get out of the Order. Or so she claimed.

"We were on the job in Lima," she said. "I waited until we took care of the target and phoned it in. We weren't supposed to be back at HQ for another week. I didn't think I'd get a better chance."

I studied her. The strong lines of her body, the softness of her face, and those eyes. I knew her tells. I saw none of them. Then again, she could've changed since the time we'd been close. She could've become an entirely different person. Looking at her now, I had to choose: act as if I believed her, or not.

She hadn't said a word yet about Faith. If she knew about me, how could she not know about Faith? She had to know.

"You want me to congratulate you on your newfound freedom?" I asked.

"I want you to say you're glad to see me," she said.

"Your coming here, making contact with me—you presence here blows my cover. If you still cared about me at all, you'd have stayed away."

"Night, the Order has no idea where you are. They don't know where I am. We're clear."

"I wish I could believe that," I said. "I've stayed alive this long by being more careful."

"Running and hiding," she said. "That's not living."

As if I didn't understand that. But running and hiding were all I had left. I had a responsibility to Faith, to keep her safe, to keep her alive. To make things possible for her that I'd never had. Would never have. Before Faith, I'd done what I had to do to stay alive. Survival had been my only concern. Now, Faith was my reason for living.

"Don't you want to know why?" Sunday asked.

"Why what?"

"Why everything," she said.

"I do." But only because it would help me to camouflage Faith and me better in yet another new city. God, I didn't want to leave Portland. Not when I'd finally felt as if I could stay somewhere.

"I couldn't live without you," Sunday said.

I raised a skeptical brow.

The corners of her mouth curved, but the smile didn't show in her eyes. "I wanted out of the Order because I was tired of the easy stuff. I wanted bigger challenges. I wanted to pick my own targets."

"That, I believe."

I understood that in the context and with the logic of my old self, my old life. My new ears listened to her words with dawning horror. She wanted to keep on killing. Not to stay alive or to have a place to belong, but for kicks. Or so she said.

She cocked her head. "Are we still friends?"

We'd shared every intimacy when we'd worked together. Now—if she told the truth—we shared a different kind of mortal danger. We'd been hunters, and now we were the hunted. And Sunday had embraced the monster inside of her. I felt cold all over.

"Why are you here?" I asked.

Heat filled her voice, rising with every syllable. "There's something magical rising in this town, something big and bad. I came to learn about it. To understand it. I came to fight it. I came to kill it."

I stared at her.

"I know you want in," she said. "We never got the chance to go up against a target like this one. It's the ultimate."

The ultimate? Whatever that meant. "No, thanks."

"The old you would've said yes in a heartbeat."

"I'm not her anymore."

My words seemed to sink in. She studied my face. "Just listen, then. Even if you won't fight with me, you should know what's here."

Faith and I wouldn't be here long enough for it to matter, but knowledge was always power. "Tell me."

"There's a Horseman of the Apocalypse in town," she said.

I blinked at her. "A what?"

"A Horseman. Like from Revelation."

I knew the Bible. My parents had been very religious. In fact, their religion had nearly killed me.

My magical knowledge base extended mostly to methods of intelligence gathering, concealment, killing, and escape. I'd come across other types of magic in my education and travels, but not as much about what Sunday suggested—that the Horsemen weren't fictional, and they weren't far-future creatures, but real in the here and now.

"The apocalypse?"

Sunday nodded.

"*The* apocalypse."

She nodded again.

The actual end of the world. Not the ramblings of cult leaders who promised their followers deliverance but ended up delivering only death. Not the fervor of those who prayed for the end times in hopes of salvation, damn the torpedoes and damn the rest of humanity so long as their asses—excuse me, souls—were saved. The actual end, breathing down our necks.

"How do you know this?" I asked.

"The signs started about a year ago. At first, I thought my imagination had gone wild, lacing together clues from unrelated occurrences. But then six months ago, a city went dark. A big city."

"Which one?" I asked.

"I can't believe you didn't notice," she said. "Houston."

Not just a big city, but the fourth largest in the country. How could I have missed that, even busy trying to stay alive and under the radar? Because I avoided everything about the place. I couldn't remember the last thing—the worst thing—that had happened to me there. The very thought of trying brought on a razor-sharp terror that started at the base of my spine and clawed its way up into my heart.

"The city going dark—the magic that caused it—was it shielded?" I asked. "Someone wanted to keep outsiders from noticing?"

If it had been, then only someone with the magical ability to see it would've caught on. Everyone else would've skipped right over it for a few days as if a city that big disappearing from the proverbial radar was perfectly normal, not worth remarking on or even having a suspicious feeling about. And once the city came back online, they'd forget that for a time it might as well have not existed.

"Yeah, it was shielded," Sunday said. "The magic that shielded it was ancient, older than anything I've ever experienced. I got lucky, noticing."

There was no such thing as luck. With Sunday, it was talent, plain and simple. And she'd followed the signs here, to a Horseman.

"Which Horseman's in town?" I asked.

Her eyes twinkled. "I'm ninety-nine percent sure that it's Death."

La Muerte? "Jesus," I said, as much in reaction to Sunday's excitement as to the identity of the big bad.

"It's like fate," she said. "Or destiny. What we are—it's like we're related to him. We're his children."

I shook my head. "What you are, maybe. I told you, I'm not who I used to be anymore."

"It's impossible to wash that much blood off your hands, Night."

"At least I'm trying."

"You let me know how that works out," she said.

I had no intention of letting her catch up with me again. "Any idea what Death looks like so I'll know if I run into him?"

"He could look like anyone at all. Anyone."

"Great," I said.

"Your sarcasm is appreciated. You have no idea how much I've missed it." She crossed her heart with her index finger for emphasis. "He's Death, Night. He could be an old lady or a teenage boy for all I know—anyone who's been touched by death closely."

"So, what kind of magic are we talking about here? Shapeshifting? Possession?"

She shrugged. "Does it matter?"

"Technically, yes," I said. "If he's shapeshifting, then he's contained in his own body and can look like anyone he wants to. If he's possessing people, then he's a free agent, so to speak, and the people he's possessing could end up messed up at best and dead at worst. It matters because given all that, if you're looking to take him out, how will you even know it's him? And are you gonna be taking out an innocent person while you're at it?"

"The old you wouldn't have cared."

"Like I keep telling you."

She sighed. "I'm not sure one innocent life outweighs a dead Horseman of the Apocalypse."

"I'm sure the innocent and their family and friends would beg to differ."

"If you're so concerned," Sunday said, "then come with me. I wasn't kidding, Night. I need you on this."

I dodged the invitation. I'd said no once, and I wouldn't say it again. What I wanted now was more information, whatever Sunday could give me that would help Faith and me survive. "Can something that old and strong even be killed?"

"I don't know, but I have to try. Night, he's *Death*. Is there anyone else I could take out that would even come close? If anyone could do it, it's me."

I agreed. Sunday killed better than anyone I'd ever seen. I'd been good at it, but Sunday was out of my league. She had courage—and bravado—that captivated as much as the rest of her, an I-don't-care-whether-I-die attitude that drew me like a moth to the flame. I hadn't cared either, once upon a time. We'd been kindred spirits. Soulmates.

She'd killed a lot of people. It didn't matter whether the people she'd killed considered themselves evil or good. It only mattered that they were dead.

I knew that better than anyone else. Sunday could lecture me about the blood on my own hands all she wanted; I knew it would drip from my fingertips until the day I died and probably flood my grave. If there was a hell separate from the ones we created for ourselves and each other in this world, I'd be sent straight there, do not pass GO. It was where I belonged.

A fucking Horseman of the Apocalypse.

I knew from my time in the Order that there had been other apocalyptic close calls—the world had almost ended half a dozen times according to the Order's records. But none of those times had involved a Horseman.

If the end of the world was really nigh this time, taking Faith and running again might not work. If something happened to her, I'd never forgive myself. If something happened to me, what would happen to Faith?

"How do you intend to find Death?" I asked.

"You don't want to help me, I don't need to tell you." She dropped her gaze from my face to the scoop neck of my T-shirt, where the pendant she'd given me hung on its delicate silver chain. "You still have it."

The silver hourglass, a symbol of what I'd been and what I'd become. I had been death itself, and I had died to that life. Now, I had a second chance that I'd sworn never to waste. A new beginning. "I've never taken it off."

She met my gaze. "Even if you won't help me, do you really want me to stay away?"

I looked into her eyes, and at her mouth. I dreamed about the shape of her mouth sometimes, the way it celebrated all her moods. Part of me wanted to kiss her and taste the fire of the life inside her and the espresso I knew she'd have sipped on waking. Part of me wanted to drown in her, for things to be like they'd been before.

"It's probably better if you do," I said.

"C'mon, Night. Reconsider."

"Thanks, but no thanks," I said with more determination than I felt.

"I hear so much as a whisper about any of the Order in town," she said, "you'll be the first to know. Same if things get out of hand with the Horseman of Death."

"Thanks," I said again.

Faith and I would have to start the motions of getting the hell out of Dodge and be gone by day after tomorrow, tops. If I could get us gone by tomorrow morning, that wouldn't be soon enough for me. But my girl wasn't ten anymore. She didn't do what I told her just because I said so. She would need a reason. I didn't want to have to tell her that I'd somehow screwed up and our cover was blown here.

"Thanks for not killing me," Sunday said.

My lips twitched into a half-smile. "You, too."

She took a hesitant step toward me, then crossed the distance in a couple of quick strides. She wrapped her arms around me and hugged me tight. Her body felt familiar, like second skin. Her strength, the amber scent in her hair, the brush of her breasts against mine. She pulled back just enough to plant a kiss on my forehead, and then one full on my lips, soft and mesmerizing.

I tasted the espresso and felt the line of the scar that ran across her bottom lip, the one that lipstick camouflaged so well. My heartbeat quickened. My arms wanted to move of their own accord, to draw her closer. I did not.

She pulled away, a question in her eyes that she asked a moment later. "Did you meet someone else? New woman? New man?"

I shook my head. "No time for love."

How could I find anything real when I had to hide my past? When I had to hide my real name? Like Faith, I'd taken a new one—Night, because I'd gone dark, inside and out. Whoever I'd been before my parents had given me to the Order, whoever I'd become under the life-or-death training the Order had given me—that girl, that woman, were dead and buried.

I'd never be able to stop running.

Sunday studied my face. Whatever she read there, she kept to herself. "Take care, Night. I'm glad you're safe," she said.

She turned away and walked out of the gym, the electronic chime announcing her departure. My heart thumped hard in my chest as she turned left into the neighborhood, disappearing from view, as the last traces of her perfume faded.

I breathed deep, making my exhales longer than my inhales, slowing my heart and recalibrating my nervous system until I felt absolutely calm, until I could think more clearly. Sunday hadn't used her magic on me, but I still felt as if I'd been run over by a forest fire.

Ten minutes until I had charge of half-awake kids here to learn how strong they could be.

Faith should've shown by now. We should've already been through the show. Her apologizing, me telling her what she could or couldn't do, her throwing back in my face that I wasn't her mother and couldn't order her around. She'd had a mother, and just because the woman had died bloody and I'd taken Faith in didn't mean I owned her. I'd heard the speech a hundred times.

Thank God Faith hadn't walked in while Sunday was here. On the heels of that thought, another.

Armageddon: coming to my backyard. As much as I couldn't take a word Sunday said as gospel, who would lie about something like that?

I stared at the door, wondering who would walk in next. The Order? The Horseman of Death?

I didn't trust Sunday as far as I could throw her.

And where in the name of everything holy was Faith?

CHAPTER 2

I TRIED TO FOCUS on the here and now: The aroma of rubber and sweat. The damp chill in the air that made my skin break out in gooseflesh. The squeak of sneakers on the floor mats and the words that rolled out of the kids' mouths that sounded to me less like words and more like distorted underwater mutterings.

With the addition of Sunday Sloan in town, the possible arrival of the Order hot on her heels, and the imminent appearance of the Horseman of Death, we'd gone far beyond whatever anxiety Faith's sneaking out in the middle of the night accounted for. The situation called for Battle Stations. Every moment that passed without Faith walking through the door ratcheted my nerves a notch tighter.

I stood near the climbing ropes, one of which currently swung under the weight of Corey Ross. Her mother thought Corey was weak and insisted that she come here three times every week to learn how to be strong. Corey was seventeen and technically old enough to tell her parents to go screw if she wanted, but in this case, she hadn't. The gym offered stability. Camaraderie. Respect. Judging from what I knew and the few offhand remarks she made about her home life, she received none of those things there.

On the other side of the rope, Jess Johnson looked up, watching

Corey's progress. Jess stood on the tips of her sneakers, adding a temporary six inches to her five feet before she lost her balance and landed flat on her soles. Her dark eyes flashed, as did the gold hoops in her ears. She'd twisted her dark, kinky curls into a loose bun on top of her head. They bounced as she moved. Her halo reminded me of a dark night out in the middle of nowhere, some place without light pollution, where the Milky Way could be seen in all its starry glory.

I'd never seen a halo like it before. It was a mystery to me, something I'd mulled over since I'd met her. Like the rest of Faith's friends, Jess had magic. Nothing dangerous that I could see. But this mystery, which had seemed like no big deal last night, only poured fuel on the fire. There were too many things going wrong. Too many coincidences.

I didn't believe in coincidences.

Jess's best friend, Ben Patterson, sixteen going on forty, stepped into my line of sight. He had wary brown eyes hidden behind a curtain of longish brown hair and even longer bangs. Most times, I saw only his thin nose and his nervous grin, the soul patch under his mouth carefully groomed. And his halo, which had all the gray color and steadfastness of a stone wall. Ben was a shield. I didn't know whether his talent only applied to him, or whether he could shield other people. Chances were good, but given his age, I'd bet he'd need to be in close proximity to them. In any normal crowd, he'd be the guy stepping between the bullied and their tormentors. He'd be the rescuer. The one everybody could count on.

He always surprised me when he opened his mouth, though I should've been used to his unusually deep voice by now.

"Who are you waiting for?" he asked.

"What makes you think I'm waiting for anyone?"

"You keep checking the door."

I sighed.

"Faith?" he asked.

I met his gaze. "You know where she's been?"

"My house," he said matter-of-factly. "But you figured that out already. It's not what you think."

"What am I thinking?"

"You're thinking sex."

What a strange thing for a boy his age to say to a woman with ten years on him, a woman in authority. And without blushing. Not even a little bit.

"It was totally not sex," he said. "We were actually studying."

At that moment, Corey shimmied down the rope, dropping to the mat underneath, between Ben and me. She grinned ear-to-ear, her heart-shaped face flushed, her forehead sheened with perspiration. The thick strands of her fire-engine red bob wilted near her face, damp from perspiration. She wore two tank tops, white on the bottom and black on the top, and long, black leggings. Most striking was her black-and-white skull cameo collection, currently occupying space on her earlobes, around her neck, and around half the fingers on each hand. Her halo shone as white as bone, and her favoring skulls made all kinds of sense. She could speak with the dead, after all. Ghosts, specifically.

"Awesome," she said.

"Yeah, you are." I raised my hand.

She high-fived me, then headed for the bathroom, where she'd left her change of clothes. Gym rags were fine here, but damned if she be caught dead in them at school.

The door chime rang. I glanced toward the front as Faith rounded the corner, half-walking, half-running across the floor, dripping water from the hem of her purple slicker, footprints puddling in her wake. The rain and caused her dark hair to curl at the ends. Her skin, normally a light, creamy brown, looked several shades paler than it ought. The halo surrounding her body had lost all of its shimmering silver depth. Now it burned orange and red with fury.

I didn't care about the anger. I cared that she was safe and that she was here.

"Hey," she said, cocking her head toward the empty back corner.

I glanced at Ben. "Y'all take a few minutes while I talk to Faith."

"No climbing until you're back," he said. "Check."

I followed Faith's wet trail to the corner into the wall of sound flowing from the speakers. I reached to turn the volume down, but stopped short when she shook her head.

She unzipped her slicker with a shower of droplets and pushed back the hood. She'd thrown on a powder blue T-shirt and a charcoal-colored sweater over top of it. A tiny silver black widow spider pendant hung at the hollow of her throat. She'd tucked her faded jeans into knee-high, black riding boots. Sometime during the night, she'd painted her fingernails black, too, and borrowed someone's black lipstick. Since Ben didn't wear that stuff, I figured she borrowed it from Corey, who did. Had Corey been at Ben's as well?

Faith closed the short distance between us and spoke low in my ear, her voice shaking. "Did you send someone to check on me this morning?"

I laid a hand on her arm. She flinched.

I pulled my hand back. "Who would I have sent? I have no friends outside of this place. Haven't been in Portland long enough."

"Red's your friend."

"Red's my boss. Makes it less likely that he'd go checking up on you as a favor to me," I said. "Honestly, I don't get why you're mad. I'm the one who should be mad, seeing as you sneaked out in the middle of the night. Not even a note. If you're gonna break the rules, Faith, at least try not to get caught."

Her mouth fell open. "You checked on me in the middle of the night."

"Every night."

"Sorry," she said, in a tone that suggested she actually meant it. "I didn't know you still did that. I don't have the nightmares anymore—not for years. You don't need to check."

"It's habit," I said. "And clearly I do."

She thinned her lips. "I'm confused. If you didn't send him, then—"

I interrupted. "Who came to see you at Ben's?"

"How did you know where I was?"

"Please," I said.

She had the grace to look a little sheepish. "This guy, he knocked on Ben's door at quarter to six, Night. White hair, pale eyes, a couple of years older than me. He said he knew you from back when, and he kept looking at me like he'd seen a ghost. Every time he opened his mouth, the wind kicked up—like, in a horror movie? He creeped the hell out of me."

She hugged herself and began to pace in three-step increments.

Someone who'd known me back when could only mean a member of the Order. But I knew every single one of them, at least up until the moment I'd made my break. I'd never met anyone matching the description Faith had given. If he was new, and he knew who Faith was, why hadn't he just killed her then and there?

"Night, he had this vibe about him. It felt like—like the night you found me."

Hiding under the bed, trembling with terror. Not knowing whether she'd be next.

She'd had terrifying dreams about that time every night for the first year she'd lived with me. She woke up screaming at 3:30 a.m. on the mark—the same time as her near-death experience—sweat-soaked and hyperventilating. Nothing soothed her except my arms around her. And time. A lot of time.

The nightmares faded, though for a while, she still came awake at the same time each night. Eventually, even that ended. I still stirred, though. I got out of bed, padding through the house on bare feet, my skin embracing summer sweat or winter chill as I checked every door and window, each corner shadow, coming to pause in the open doorway to her bedroom. I watched her sleep for five, ten minutes, grateful for the peace that showed on her face most of the time.

I wished for peace in my own heart. It never came—nor, if I were honest with myself, should it. I hadn't felt a single lick of remorse all the years that I'd killed. But since then, regret had taken up residence inside my heart and showed no signs of leaving. I wished for a way to make things right. I wished for some way to ensure that all those deaths at my hands—that those people had not died in vain.

I had my own bad dreams. In them, I saw the faces of every single person I'd killed. I felt them die, and I felt pieces of them—their loves, their memories—fall into me. They shouted their pain and their anguish, their joy and their love. The sound became a cacophony inside my head. At the end, always, they screamed at me to remember the one thing I could not. That one elusive memory. The one thing that could heal—or destroy—me.

Maybe I deserved to be destroyed. But this wasn't about what I deserved. It was about Faith. She should never have to relive the night her parents died.

I rubbed the bridge of my nose. "That guy said he knew me."

Faith stopped pacing and nodded.

"I don't know him."

"Are you sure?" she asked. "Are you sure he wasn't there that night?"

"I'm sure," I said. "

"Then who was he?"

"I'm gonna find out."

"With what? Your private-eye superpowers? You're a gym coach. With exceptional intuition."

"Please," I said.

I was more than that, and she knew it. She knew all about my magic. She just didn't know how I'd honed it, how I'd used it before I found her.

"What am I supposed to do in the meantime, Night?"

"You can't go to school," I said.

Her shoulders sank halfway to their usual place. "If he knew where to find me this morning, he'd know to find me there. Or here, for that matter."

"Yes, but here you've got people."

"Red, again."

I nodded. Red had magic. He didn't think anyone knew that. He tried to hide it, and mostly, he did. But no one could hide the flavor of their magic from me, not when I could see it plain and clear in their halos.

Red's halo never varied: grass green and earth brown. Comforting. Protective. And that was what and who he was. He saw the good in people where others would see only trouble.

"Red's office," I said.

Faith met my gaze. "You sure he won't mind? Like you said, he's your boss."

"He likes you," I said.

"You mean he likes you." She waggled a brow, changing the tone of the conversation on a dime.

"He's good to work for," I said.

"You know that's not what I meant."

Didn't I? I didn't want to go a round or ten about Red and how we danced around each other, especially not with my girl. If it were up to her, she'd pair me off with the first decent man or woman, and we'd be a happily-ever-after family. Her hope sprang eternal.

"I'll call the school and tell them you're sick. You can pick up your homework later from the electronic drop box," I said.

"That's called changing the subject, Night."

"Pot calling the kettle. He flirts," I said. "It's no big deal."

"You flirt back," she said. "So it kind of is."

I pointed at the office. "Go."

She marched off, turning her head toward Ben and Jess as she did. I couldn't see Faith's face, but I could see Jess's, and the concern in Jess's eyes.

Jess mouthed something at Faith that looked like *Him?*

Faith shrugged.

Watching all of that, piecing it together with Ben's weird comments about Faith not having been sleeping with him, that she'd been over studying but managed to paint her fingernails with something only Corey would wear—it added up to a teenage conspiracy.

It might have something to do with the other thing that bothered me. Something Faith had not said before she'd walked away.

In the past, any potential threat had been grounds to pack up and move right then and there, no questions asked. Early in our time together, she'd done what I'd asked in that department without hesitation. After a couple of years, as her night terrors subsided, she put up more of a fight, though she'd still gone along. It was so hard to be the new kid all the time, to try to make friends, only to find that as soon as you'd made a place for yourself, you had to let it go. It was hard to lose like that.

I hated that it had to be done, but I made it happen anyway. Better to be heartsore and alive than to stay in one place too long and end up six feet under.

All of that was why I hadn't wanted to have to tell her we had to run again. But given what happened this morning at Ben's house, she should've at least asked what I thought.

She knew I had to be thinking about it. A mysterious white-haired guy who claimed to know me from before, and who'd shown up on her friend's doorstep at the crack of dawn? That was textbook for *time to run again*.

Add to that everything that had already happened this morning and what in God's name was going on?

Ben's deep voice busted up my thoughts. "Hey, Night? My turn, yeah?"

I sent him an automatic grin that, judging by the frown he answered with, did not resemble an actual smile. I shook it off and made my way back to the ropes.

"Get it," I said.

He handed Jess his mug and started up the rope.

She took a sip and grimaced. "He likes coffee with his sugar."

"I commiserate," I said.

She studied my face. Whatever she saw there, she couldn't keep it out of her expression. Mouth turned down. Eyes narrowed. Finally, she looked everywhere but at me.

Once Ben came down from the rope, he spent the remainder of the session studying his mug or his shoes, unwilling to say anything else embarrassing—or anything at all. I clapped him between the shoulder blades as we said good-bye and he strolled out the door into the rain.

Jess slung her backpack over her shoulder, holding the door open for Corey, now spiffy in her short, dark blue, pleated plaid dress and matching plaid tights. The dark still held sway outside, but the light had changed, the glow of the streetlights not quite so bright now that the rising sun filtered slowly through clouds.

Jess let the other girl slip out, waving after her. "I'll catch up," she said.

"Don't be late!" Corey called back. Her footfalls on the wet pavement faded as she walked away.

Jess let go of the door and turned to face me as it closed. "You're not what I was told you were."

Her words took me by surprise. "What's that, Jess?"

"A stone cold killer."

Just like that. Matter-of-fact, like her best friend, Ben. "Who told you that?"

"My aunt," she said.

Her aunt. I'd never met the woman. If she'd told Jess I was a killer, then the aunt knew more about me than I did about her. "Outside."

Jess stepped out as I asked. I followed her and waited the few seconds for the door shut behind us. Faith was still in Red's office. Let her stay there until I knew more about what we were up against in Jess's aunt.

The mist had morphed into soft rain. Across the street at the coffee shop, someone laughed in short bursts that reminded me of a barking seal.

"Why would you say that to me?" I asked. "Why would your aunt say it about me?"

"We know about your magic." Jess hitched her backpack higher on her shoulder. "You're the dark side, Night. The flavor of your magic, everything about you. We knew when you came to town. We felt you arrive. You're unmistakable."

"Not to most people." Most of the people I'd killed had never seen or heard me coming. The Order hadn't caught up with me yet as far as I could tell—though Sunday had. And Sunday was a special case.

Jess shook her head. "We're not most people."

Had Jess and her people—she'd said *we*—felt Sunday arrive in town as well? If there was the slightest chance, I'd need to get word to Sunday. Otherwise, she'd have a target on her back and not know it until too late. Even if she was still a killer. Even if she was crazy.

Sunday had been a light for me in the darkness. That mattered more.

"Enlighten me," I said. "Who are you?"

"We're the magical law in this town."

I'd come across several types of magical law enforcement in my life. The world was full of them because magical beings, human and not remotely human, walked the Earth all the time. Most people didn't notice. They went about their lives blissfully unaware that the shade of a dead person followed them, or that the hot girl dancing in the club who made them want to fuck was a faery or a demon, or that the girl who rang up their groceries when they had too many to use the self-service checkout station dabbled in the kind of magic that would curl their hair.

Most people didn't know the Order existed. Or that the assassins in its employ had been born with magical abilities and brought into service as children because their parents couldn't deal with objects flying around the house every time their child threw a tantrum or the idea that their child spoke to spirits—especially if something seemed to answer.

From personal experience, I understood that most parents couldn't handle being made to see and hear things, or understanding that their child had caused them to do so, or believing a demon had possessed their child and that no amount of torturous exorcism could excise it.

But there were people who did see and hear and know. And those people had gradually evolved to act as a counterweight to perceived—and sometimes, actual—threat. Faery seers policed the fae beings who entered the human world. They also took on demons and angels, both the humanized half-breeds and the full-blooded, full-powered deep dwellers of hells and heavens. Some witches and other human magical practitioners set themselves up as guardians of cities or wild lands. They tracked magical creatures who entered their territory and meted out justice or retribution to those who committed magical crimes. They made a habit of running undesirables out of town.

On occasion, the Order had functioned as a kind of policing body when beings that were too powerful to walk the human world entered it and refused to leave. Of course, the Order did that by taking jobs to assassinate those beings. It was rare, but it happened.

Jess claimed to be in service of the law. She'd accused me of murder.

"Which kind of law?" I asked. "What authority are you claiming?"

"Watchers," she said. "We're Watchers."

I'd heard of them in my training with the Order, but I'd never seen one in real life. My mentor in the Order told me that if they'd ever existed at all, they'd gone extinct. I could see now that he'd lied.

The original Watchers had been descendants of the Nephilim, or fallen angels. The angels mated with humans and the offspring became known as Watchers because they could see magic that humans could not and they could perform certain types of magic as well. As far as other humans were concerned, the Watchers were gods. That didn't sit well with human priests, who claimed it didn't sit well with their capital-G God. Supposedly, that had been the impetus for unleashing the Biblical flood upon the world as a punishment. Supposedly, it redeemed the transgression of those humans who mated with the angels, and cleansed the world of those Watcher offspring.

Clearly also a lie, because the girl standing in front of me claimed to be one.

"If you believe I'm a threat," I said, "I should be treated as one."

"That's what my aunt said. But I don't buy it. And no, I wasn't supposed to say any of this to you at all, but I couldn't just stand by and watch it go down."

"What's that?" I folded my arms across my chest.

"My aunt wants you dead. She thinks you're bringing the big one down on us. We can't have him here. He'll destroy us. He'll destroy this town, and he won't stop there."

Her aunt wanted me dead. I'd never met the woman. As far as I knew, I'd never done a damned thing to her or to her kin. This was about what she thought I might do. "You're gonna have to be more specific about who you mean," I said, although I had a hunch, given what Jess and her people were descended from.

"The Horseman of Death. The Angel of Death."

Two different beings? No, the same one. The Horsemen *were* angels in service of God in bringing on the apocalypse and seeing it through. Second time I'd heard the Angel of Death's name in as many hours. "The big one?"

Jess shifted her weight from one foot to the other. "He's the most powerful angel in our lore, and he's invisible to us. We can see everything else magical, but he could sneak up on us and we wouldn't even know it."

"I'll bet that's terrifying," I said.

"You have no idea."

Everyone was different. I couldn't walk in Jess's shoes, but I understood some things about bone-deep fear. "Your aunt on her way here to take me out?" I asked.

"Not yet. There's something she has to take care of first."

"Calling in reinforcements? I'm not easy to get rid of. Do yourself a favor and don't try."

Jess curled her hands into fists. "Stop it. Stop acting like I'm, like I'm…."

I finished her sentence for her. "The enemy?"

"Yes," she said. "I'm trying to warn you, Night. I like you. I don't think you're as bad as my aunt says. And I don't think you're the reason the Angel of Death is heading our way."

I took a deep breath and blew it out slowly. "Why not?"

"Because if you wanted to hurt any one of us by now, you'd have done it. And because of Faith," Jess said. "If you were a killer, Faith wouldn't love you so much."

If Jess only knew the whole story, she might change her mind. "How many Watchers are coming for me?"

"Just my aunt. She's all that's left here in the city, at least until I grow into my magic all the way."

Which meant there were others around the world who could be

called if needed. "What's the one thing she has to do first before she comes after me?"

As soon as I asked the question, the answer popped into my mind.

Jess's words echoed my thoughts. "She's got to get Faith to a safe place."

"Your aunt lays a finger on my kid—"

"Please don't hurt her, Night."

I studied Jess's face. I saw no secrets there. She'd shared everything she'd been told, which made it likely she hadn't been told everything.

"You know, you're lucky," I said. "You were raised in a magical family, one that understands your gifts and appreciates them. A lot of us don't have that. Instead, we get superstitious priests called on us, beaten, locked away, thrown out. Our parents don't know what's the matter with us. They only know that we're wrong. That we're evil. That's what they think. And there's no reporting what's done to us to Child Services or the cops. The magic we carry keeps that from happening. We're rendered invisible. Helpless."

"I'm sorry," she said.

"Don't be sorry—wake up. Faith is with me because I took her out of a home where all of that was happening to her."

"Thank you for taking her," Jess said. "I think my aunt knows that, but it doesn't change what she thinks."

I doubted Jess knew everything her aunt thought. I posed the question I'd asked Jess before, this time with a different meaning. "Why'd you say all of this?"

"I can't be everything to everybody," she said. "My aunt wants one thing. My friends want something else. Push. Pull. I never get to choose. This morning, I am."

I understood all too well what it felt like to have to do that. "What are you choosing, Jess?"

"The right thing," she said.

I nodded. "Then answer one question for me: Is there a kid a little older than you with white hair among your number? A Watcher?"

"No," she said. "I told you, it's just me and my aunt in Portland."

I held her gaze. "All of this has something to do with why y'all were at Ben's last night. This is connected with the Angel of Death."

She clammed up fast. "I should go."

"You don't want to be late, like Corey told you," I said.

She turned on her heel and walked away.

I knew where she lived. I'd head there shortly, to talk with the aunt. Know your enemy. And gather as much intel as possible, because even if Faith and I ran, these Watchers might follow.

I'd go as soon as Red arrived to look after Faith. I didn't want to leave Faith alone, but I couldn't take her with me.

I turned to go back inside only to see her standing on the other side of the door, palms pressed flat against the glass. Eavesdropping. I'd bet a cool million she'd heard every word spoken between Jess and me. Her halo had flashed back to spark-filled red, heating up by the second. She looked ready to explode.

CHAPTER 3

FAITH LOOKED AT me with wary eyes. She didn't move an inch as I approached the door, only pressed her hands harder into the glass, bleaching her palms white. She'd shrugged off her slicker and tucked the curled ends of her hair behind her ears, I saw. Droplets of rain still clung to the tops of her riding boots.

"Back up," I said.

She did, just far enough for me to squeeze inside.

The classic rock playlist I'd started out with earlier had run its course, giving way to the old-school Michael Jackson streaming through the speakers. The rubber on the floor squeaked under the newly wet soles of my sneakers. In addition to its thick scent, I smelled feet. A quick look toward the cubbies showed me why: a pair of sweaty socks had spilled out of Ben's pack onto the floor. He hadn't noticed.

I moved to pick them up. Faith stepped in front of me and folded her arms across her chest. I tried to go around her. She sidestepped to block my path.

"It's not what you think," she said.

"You and the others aren't trying to work some kind of magic against the Angel of Death?"

She blanched.

"I think I hit that one out of the park," I said.

"This isn't how I wanted you to find out."

"You planned to tell me?" I asked.

She nodded. "It's just—we're still working on a theory, on logistics—and I wanted to wait until we had something real before I opened my mouth. Jess screwed that up."

"She didn't say anything about what you were working on."

"She said enough."

"You overhear all of it? How about the part where her aunt wants me dead?"

Faith fisted her hands in her hair. "I swear I didn't know. I thought it was me."

I narrowed my eyes. "What?"

"Jess never wanted me to go near her place. At first, I figured she was keeping me away from whatever Watcher magic was going on over there, like it was a trust thing. I had to earn it, and then she'd let me in. And then she opened up in a lot of other ways. We're friends. We're tight. But she still wouldn't let me come over, and the way she talked about her aunt was all one-word answers in sharp tones. I thought her aunt didn't like me."

I followed the logic, even if it was incomplete. "You never wondered whether they had something to hide?"

"Why would Jess hide anything from me?" she asked.

Because they were friends. They were tight. "You put a lot of trust in her and the others. Too much."

"I told you. We're friends."

She'd never really had friends, not like these. I understood the hell out of that.

"What about you?" she asked. "You looked crazy worried when I got here. Now you look like a cornered animal. What gives?"

I ticked off the trouble on my fingers. "The Angel of Death and the bloodthirsty aunt."

She met my gaze. "And the past? It's come back to haunt us again?"

Sunday. The Order. People we ran from. People who wanted her dead.

I nodded.

She took that in, moving to lean against the wall and folding her arms across her chest. When she spoke, her voice came out small and quiet. "I know what you're gonna suggest, and the answer is no."

No, she didn't want to leave.

"I don't even want to talk about it," she said.

"I understand," I said.

"How could you?" she asked. "You never act like it's a big deal, leaving one place and going to another. You never act like starting over hurts."

Because I had her welfare to worry about first. Because it hurt less to start over if you never put down roots. Because I'd never known any other way.

"Is this home?" I asked.

"Yes," she said.

"You want to make a stand? Even if it turns out badly?"

She mulled my question. "If that doesn't happen here, it will somewhere else."

"You're right," I said.

"I am?" She stared at me.

"I don't think running is gonna solve our problems this time. I think we have to stay."

Faith breathed in deep, then exhaled a shaky breath. "What do we do?"

"First we figure out why the world seems to be falling down all over us." I had a hunch about what had started the avalanche. "I need you to answer a question for me, Faith."

She waited.

"How much magic have you been using, working on all the Angel of Death stuff with your friends?"

"Why?"

"It's not a trick question," I said.

She studied her boots. "None."

"You sure about that?"

"If I use my magic, then the odds that someone from the past could find me get higher. The odds that someone else bad will find me get higher," she said. "I know. You drilled it into me."

"I wish I never had to."

"I know," she said.

Before we'd moved to Portland, she'd used her power only twice. The first time, I'd found out just in time that the Order was breathing down our necks. The second time, it'd been a disaster of almost deadly proportions. Since then, she'd kept her magic locked down. But temptation was strong. Stronger, the need to fit in.

If Jess was a budding Watcher, Corey could speak with the dead, and Ben was a shield, Faith would want to contribute. She had the kind of power that would wow the others, the kind of power that someone had paid the Order to take out of this world because they considered Faith too dangerous to be allowed to live.

Faith could talk to gods. She could hear them speak back to her.

There were a lot of gods in the world, some of them more powerful than others. Some who never walked among humans, and others who did. The gods were territorial. They stuck to places and people they liked and/or felt responsibility toward.

Faith had found a god once—or one had found her. The god hadn't harmed her, but connecting with Faith lit her up like a neon sign to those looking for her. For us. We'd barely made it out of the city alive.

If Faith had pushed that memory away, if she'd felt compelled to help or wanted a greater sense of belonging—who could resist that? Her friends were doing it. And if they were, their magic should provide some cover for hers.

"How are you helping your friends with Death if you're not using your powers?" I asked.

"I run errands," she said.

"Shoe leather express?"

"And my bike."

"What else?"

She shifted her weight from one foot to the other. "I help brainstorm."

"Faith—"

"All right," she said. "I used it a little bit, just to check out who's here. I was in a protective circle and I was with a bunch of other people with magic. No one found out. I was, like, invisible."

I closed my eyes so tight, I saw bursts of purple and red on the insides of my eyelids.

"What?" she asked.

I looked at her. At the fear that tugged her eyes wider and pulled at the corners of her mouth. "It's not your fault. It's mine. Not using your power keeps you invisible. You tamped it down and after a while, I could pretend that everything was normal. That we're normal."

"What's the bad?" she asked.

"It kept you ignorant."

"I'm not—"

"Not like that," I interrupted. "You're whip-smart, Faith, and you're a survivor. But because I didn't want you using your magic, I didn't teach you much about it."

She dropped her arms to her sides. "But I know how it works."

"Yeah," I said. "But you don't know about the consequences. The way some people use magic to hunt others, for instance. You know what a magical signature is?"

She shook her head.

"It's a flavor that's unique to your magic. Even if you hid in a crowd of a hundred people—a thousand—someone looking for that flavor could zero in on you. Sure, those people provide interference, but not for long."

Her eyes grew wider. "How long, Night?"

I sighed. "How many times did you use your magic? It wasn't just a little, was it?"

"It was at first. But then, nothing bad happened, so I kept on. Like, nine, maybe ten times."

"That's more than enough."

"Oh, God," she said.

"It's not your fault," I repeated, slowly and clearly. "You didn't know."

"I should've," she said.

"Now you do, so you can do better from here on out."

She shook her head. "Does that even matter?" she asked. "If I get us caught—or worse—"

"We'll deal with it," I said.

She looked at my face and I could see she knew I meant it.

The door opened behind me. The chime sliced all the way to the heart of my ramped-up nerves. I jumped a half-inch as the chill damp rushed in, along with the strong smell of coffee and a whiff of tea tree shampoo.

Red had arrived.

His gravelly voice rolled over me, his southeast Texas accent faint but recognizable. "What's wrong?"

I turned around slowly. "Nothing."

He met my gaze with sharp green eyes, their corners crinkled with concern, his brow furrowing to match. Silver hair, shaggy and damp, brushed his shoulders. His silver mustache had the same scraggly look. He wasn't old enough to have hair that color, and I'd told him so; he was only a couple of years older than me. He'd replied that his hair had started to turn when he was the ripe old age of sixteen. He'd had a shock to his system. He hadn't elaborated.

This morning, he wore a pair of long, dark blue gym pants and a dark gray hoodie, unzipped just enough to show the collar of his white T-shirt and the very top of a tattoo on his chest—the fiery crown of a red heart wreathed in white and red roses, a symbol of the Catholicism he'd since given up. He wore black leather fingerless gloves, which he began to peel off, and he'd dragged in a soggy mat of fallen brown and gold leaves on the bottoms of his white sneakers. His halo was, as always solid, earthen.

"Doesn't look like nothing," he said, his accent growing a little thicker. "Well, you look all right, Night, but Faith here looks like the world's about to end."

His presence, his voice—everything about him—made me feel like

I belonged. Just like his gym did, and, if I were honest, Red more than anything or anyone else was responsible for making me feel like I'd found something I didn't want to lose.

"I'm glad to see you," I said. "I need to run a quick errand. Can you keep an eye on Faith while I'm gone?"

He looked from me to Faith and back again. "You planning on telling me why?"

I didn't want to, but I didn't have much of a choice. Red would be on the Watchers' radar, too, but in his case, that was probably no big deal since he helped people. But the Order wouldn't care about that. They'd figure he knew something about me and they'd do whatever they felt they needed to in order to extract information from him. And Sunday? Who the hell knew? On top of that, the Angel of Death was in town for God only knew what and God only knew why, and Red deserved to know that. I just didn't want him to know it yet, at least not until I had more information to give him.

"It's our mess," I said. "Give us a chance to clean it up first?"

He studied me. Unlike me, he didn't have a poker face. And despite my not giving away a single thing by my expression, he'd read between the lines of what I'd said more deeply than I wanted, and it was written all over his eyes and the set of his mouth. "How long do you think you'll need?"

"Couple of hours," I said.

He nodded. "All right."

"Thanks," I said. I looked at Faith, hoping she'd understand the question I asked with my eyes. Since she'd heard every word of my conversation with Jess, she'd know more than anyone what I would do next, why I needed to get it done.

She didn't nod or say anything at all. Instead, she looked at the floor.

I walked toward the back of the gym to grab my pack and shrug on my hoodie. When I turned around, Faith had disappeared into Red's office, but Red stood in the same spot, hands shoved in the pockets of his pants.

I met his gaze and held it as I walked back toward him, stopping only when I came very close and we stood toe-to-toe. This close, I felt something besides the impulse to survive. I felt him and his green and earth halo and his steadfast see-the-good-in-people trained on me—and something else, something primal flowing off of him and through me. A desire to protect. And just plain desire.

A flutter in my chest—and the same flutter lower down—answered. I kept any sign of it off of my face. I couldn't open that door, not for real. Not with anyone. Flirting was one thing. Flirting was just play, and sometimes play could help you get what you wanted. Sex—or more than that—was something else entirely, and not a risk I could take with so much at stake.

"You want to tell me where you're going?" he asked softly, keeping the words between us. Even if Faith stood at the office door, she was unlikely to hear anything except our voices.

Did he know what Jess was? What her aunt was? I thought he might have a clue if not the whole picture, but either way, I didn't have the luxury of launching into an explanation right this minute, not if I wanted to have any hope of the element of surprise with Jess's aunt.

Jess had warned me against her aunt's wishes, thinking that was the best way to go about saving both me and her aunt. She might be having second thoughts if she hadn't already. I wanted to arrive at the house before her conscience hounded her into confessing what she'd said.

"Not really," I said. "At least not right now."

"Text me if you think you'll be late. Or if anything goes wrong."

I raised a brow. "Wrong?"

"This isn't any run-of-the-mill mess, and you're leaving your daughter in my care."

I nodded. "We'll talk when I get back."

He watched me walk out, the chime announcing my departure. My relief on clearing the door, then turning north to walk down the street to my car, was enormous. My instinct, the animal inside of me, felt like a live wire, but my frontal lobes began to reassert themselves so I could feel something besides fear and the desperate need to survive, so I could think about what to say to Jess's aunt and what to do besides rely on my assassin's training to eliminate her as a threat.

The mist thickened to steady drops of rain that began to soak through my hood. A line of cars rolled past, tires kicking up spray, headlights puncturing the gloom. The wind gusted, rattling the branches of Japanese maples and the lone mimosa under which I'd parked my old blue Honda. Sliding into the front seat, I caught a whiff of stale corn chips and Sunday's amber and vanilla perfume.

She'd been in my car. Not exactly a surprise, except for the timing. If I could still smell her scent, she'd been in here within the last hour at the outside, and probably closer to the last half-hour.

I checked the glove box, riffling through old parking meter receipts, petrified protein bars, and basic gear—tire pressure gauge, extra batteries, travel packs of tissues. I got out and checked under the seats, kneeling on the street and soaking through the knees of my pants. I went over the trunk. All the usual stuff remained—couple of blankets, a few bottles of water, first aid kit. The spare tire and the jack were where they were supposed to be. I looked under the car. No tracking devices. Nothing suspicious.

Sunday had searched the vehicle, but she hadn't altered it in any way. She'd done it to get a bead on me. And to let me know she'd invaded more of my private space, my new life.

Slipping back into the car, I gripped the wheel hard enough to bleach my knuckles. My breath fogged the air, and in a minute the windshield would begin to fog, too. I started the engine and turned on the defroster as the wind gusted again. The mimosa's branches scraped the roof like bony fingers.

Whatever Sunday had said to me this morning about staying away, she clearly hadn't meant it. Maybe she sat in another vehicle on the street, waiting for me to pull out into traffic so she could follow.

In the pocket of my hoodie, my phone buzzed and chimed—incoming text from Faith, forwarding me Jess's home address from the gym's records.

I scanned the cars I could see in front and behind, on the opposite side of the road, all of them empty. I took no comfort in that. Pulling into the street, I took more care than I usually did to check for tails. If Sunday was back there somewhere, I couldn't spot her. In fact, with the rain coming down, it was harder to see what I needed in order to drive the two miles south and east to Jess's house, heading south past restaurants and coffee shops to Stark, then east past expensive houses and Laurelhurst Park, with its tall, exquisite Douglas firs and walking trails, plus a playground and basketball court.

The North Tabor neighborhood was filled with the kinds of houses I'd want to have for Faith and me—two stories, porches big enough for swings and plants, backyards ripe for vegetable gardens. The streets were lined with more maples and ginkgo trees that had shed their leaves, transforming sidewalks into carpets of red and gold. The neighborhood was quiet and dotted with great spots for pancakes and burgers. One day. If we lived through what was coming and made it clean out the other side, one day. Also, I'd need to win the lottery. It could happen.

I parked in front of Jess's house, rain pouring down as I climbed the front steps. The yard was a tall, steep slope filled with lavender and rosemary that had been allowed to grow into the space allocated for the steps. The stalks brushed against my legs, releasing calming and medicinal fragrances, and telling me something important about Jess's aunt. As beautiful as they were, lavender and rosemary were magically protective plants, serving to cleanse anyone who passed through the yard and to frighten away anyone who approached with ill intent.

The house itself was a double-decker painted buttercream yellow with white trim. Twinkling lights hung in both of the picture windows, framing a view into the living room on the right and the dining room on the left. I didn't see anyone inside, but I caught a glimpse of a glow emanating from the room behind the living area.

The wide, high-railed wooden porch held two oversized wicker chairs in cheerful red with white cushions and a matching wicker table in between. A huge tuxedoed tomcat with muddy paws sat on the rail, following my every move until I stepped onto the thirsty mat in front of the door, at which point he leapt down onto the white porch boards and slinked away, leaving a trail of fat footprints in his wake.

I rang the bell. Footfalls sounded on the hardwood floor inside, drawing nearer to the door, which swung open on hinges that creaked haunted-house style.

The woman who stood at the threshold looked me up and down, and I did the same to her.

She could've been anyone. Any human anyone. But her halo held the night sky, like Jess's—and flashed blue fire so brightly that for a moment I could hardly see her. Then the light dimmed and I got a good look at the woman—the Watcher—who wanted to see me dead and take my child.

CHAPTER 4

SHE LOOKED HARMLESS. Emphasis on *looked*.

Jess's aunt had dark brown skin and brown eyes that shaded from kind to suspicious in a heartbeat. She wore her hair in a bun, clear gloss on her lips, and silver-framed glasses on her nose. She had on a green sweatshirt with red velvet trim at the collar, cuffs, and hem. Darth Vader's mask featured on the front, with words underneath that said *I find your lack of holiday cheer disturbing*. She'd completed her outfit with a pair of faded jeans that were worn at the knees. Her feet were bare.

"You got a pair on you, coming here," she said.

She filled the doorway, blocking not only my path, but my view into the yellow house. Her voice reminded me of my own *abuela*, who'd smoked most of her life, but quit on her sixtieth birthday. Jess's aunt looked only to be about fifty.

A tantalizing scent wafted from behind her, sparking a memory so strong that it made my knees weak: chiles and chicken and tomatillos. I'd smelled lots of Tex-Mex in my time, but there was something about the particular combination of ingredients that triggered my senses. Something personal to me.

"I believe in sizing up my enemies," I said.

"My niece said something to you," the aunt said. "Don't act like she didn't. No other reason you'd be here. Yesterday, you had no idea we existed. Otherwise, you'd have dropped by sooner. Am I right?"

I nodded.

"You only wanted a look at me, or did you have something else in mind?" she asked.

"Door number two."

"You want to come in, then?"

"You'd have a monster like me in?" I asked.

"Not unless you agree to the ground rules. I give you guest rights, and you promise not to engage in any violence."

Offering me guest rights meant taking responsibility for whatever happened to me. If harm came to me, then it would be as if harm came to my hostess. In times gone by, whoever caused the harm would be punished as if they'd raised a hand to the mistress of the house. In this case, any wrong done to me would be visited on her as well.

"Seems fair."

"No lies, neither. Not from you and not from me."

I nodded.

She frowned. "I'm Addie."

"Night."

"I know your name. Wipe your feet and take off your shoes in the foyer." She turned on her heel and walked back from where she'd come—the room with the light shining from it.

As I stepped inside, I realized what that room was: the kitchen. The spicy scent that poured from it enveloped me in the long arms of my distant past. Before I knew it, my mouth began to water. Not conducive to strong negotiations, but I couldn't deny the hunger that grew in my belly, and it was hunger for more than food. It was hunger for the lost pieces of myself.

I shook off that feeling. I could indulge it later. After I left the house of my would-be murderer.

I kicked off my sneakers and left them by the door beside the collection of fuzzy house slippers, rain boots, and hikers neatly placed in a three-story shoe rack. I pushed my hood back and unzipped the hoodie, surveying the living room.

Two cocoa-colored suede couches framed the space, a long, scarred, oak coffee table between them. A chocolate-brown sisal rug cradled the furniture. There was a fireplace behind glass doors, with gas flames dancing inside. Its warmth filled the room. On the mantel, pictures of Jess, some of the girl alone and a couple with her aunt. A dark TV screen was bolted to the wall above them.

On my left, a round, distressed-wood dining table had been painted black and circled with black stools instead of chairs. In the center of the table, a shiny silver bowl barely contained an avalanche of bright orange clementines. There wasn't an ounce of dust on any of it, but neither did it appear to be well-loved. That table was for company.

Addie called from the kitchen. "You coming?"

I padded across the hardwood in my sock feet, getting a feel for the place. Unlike with people, most places didn't have halos of their own, emphasis on the word *most*. The lavender and rosemary—or some spell—shielded the halo from my sight outside, but now that I was through the door, I could see the same blue fire that Addie gave off covering the walls and floor and ceiling. It was thicker near openings to the outside world—the fireplace, the windows, the doors. In places, it coiled out toward me as I passed, tendrils of blue flame brushing my cheeks and shoulders, taking my temperature, assessing my character.

I stepped into the kitchen, the wood floors shifting to tile. The room held a collection of stainless steel appliances and a garden window over the sink with a riot of starter herbs in tiny clay pots. There was a worn oak breakfast table in the corner by the back door, with a tray in the center that cradled salt and pepper shakers, a caddy of silverware, and a stack of white paper napkins. The floor near it was as well-traveled as the table was well-used. This was the center of the home, right here.

A large soup pot filled with the mouthwatering, memory-triggering substance simmered on the stovetop. Addie stood in front of it, ladling the contents into first one soup bowl and then another.

"Hope you're hungry," she said, handing me a bowl and a spoon.

"It's too early for lunch." I stared at what she'd handed me. It wasn't at all complicated for having caused such a sensory triggering inside of me. It was *posole*. It smelled exactly the way my *abuela*'s had smelled. She liked to make it when the fall days finally brought cool enough air to make her want to pull on a sweater.

"I know," Addie said. "But it's never too early for memories. I felt compelled to buy these ingredients yesterday and I had no idea why, but I've learned when instinct tells me something that clearly, I ought to just go ahead and do what it says. So if you're wondering, you caught me by surprise, but only a little. I figured someone would be coming. Didn't know it'd be you."

I followed her to the table and sat my bowl and myself down. Steam rose from the *posole*. "You cook for all the people you want to kill?"

"It's a kind of divination," she said.

I got the impression that if I were someone else, she would've made up some excuse instead of telling me what she was after. But since I already knew her endgame, she felt no need to lie to me about that.

"What will it tell you?" I asked.

"Who your people are."

I understood from the way she said the words that by *people* she meant *family*. "I don't have family of blood, only of choice."

"You wouldn't be the first," she said, and dug into her bowl.

"I didn't summon the Angel of Death," I said.

She grabbed a napkin from the stack. "You don't have to summon him for him to come for you."

"There's nothing special about me. I may have been the monster you think I am at one point, but I've reformed. I've got nothing to offer him."

"Except the blood on your hands," she said.

"Which makes me no more special than any other killer."

She cocked her head. "You really don't know why the Angel would be coming for you, do you?"

"No," I said.

I dipped my spoon into the *posole* and tasted. The flavor exploded in my mouth—the heat from the chiles, the brightness of the tomatillos, the comforting richness of the chicken, which had been roasted first, and the chewiness of the hominy. There was white rice in there, too, and the broth was homemade from the roasted chicken carcass. I didn't have to have seen Addie cook it to know that. The recipe she'd used and wherever she'd gotten it—whatever entity had given her the marching orders?—was the same one my *abuela* used.

I glanced at Addie to find her staring at me expectantly. "It's delicious."

She narrowed her eyes, and I saw she wasn't staring *at* me but *around* me, looking for the information about my people, or something else. Either she didn't like what she saw or—

"I don't understand," she said.

I raised a brow.

"There's nothing there."

"I told you I don't have family of blood."

"You have blood family who loved you, though. At least one, somewhere, some time."

I shook my head.

"There is literally no one who watches over you from beyond the grave, and no hint that anyone wishes to. That, I've never seen," she said.

"So?"

"So it's a wonder that you're still alive. And it's no wonder you became what you are."

I set down my spoon. "Are we finished psychologizing me?"

"We can talk about something else if you like," she said. "How about Faith?"

I didn't like the sound of that name rolling from Addie's mouth. "I hear you want to take her away from me."

"You're not qualified to watch over her," Addie said. "We are."

"Explain."

"She's far more than just a little girl. She's a conduit to the divine."

"A conduit?"

"She can talk to the divine. Speak to the divine. Do you know how rare that is? There's no one else who can do that—no one else we're aware of, at any rate. She can't be allowed to use that power in inappropriate and dangerous ways. She must be controlled."

"Controlled?" An interesting choice of words. "She's a teenager. There's no such thing as ruling her. It's impossible. She'll make mistakes—she's made plenty already, just like the rest of us. She knows right from wrong. She's a good kid. But she's nobody's servant."

"I don't mean for her to be a servant," Addie said. "I mean for her to be a tool."

Anger bubbled in my gut, simmering on a slow boil. I'd taken her from a prison imposed on her by people who supposedly loved her. I'd be damned if I'd allow her ever to be treated that way again.

I leaned back in my chair. "What do you plan to use her for?"

"To talk to God," Addie said.

Addie was a Watcher, which by definition meant she was descended from beings God did not approve of. "What would you want to do that for?"

"To declare our loyalty and ask for instructions," she said.

"For what?"

"For the coming war."

"You mean the apocalypse."

She nodded. "We're claiming Faith for our side. Now that she's within our reach, we can do that. Before, things weren't so clear cut. They were…murkier. She was a danger."

A danger who couldn't be allowed to use her power in inappropriate ways. Hazardous ways. The only way to ensure that someone didn't use their power was to take it away. There was only one way to separate someone with magic from their power: kill them.

I had a sudden intuition, the kind born out of instinct. No matter how much I wanted to be ruled by some other, more rational, civilized part of my mind these days, I couldn't ignore that kind of thing. That kind of knowing was always true.

"You went after her before," I said.

"We did what we thought was right and necessary," Addie said.

The slow boil in my gut became a fury. Since when was killing a child right or necessary? "When? How did you do it?"

"It was before you knew her."

Before meant that Faith had been with her parents, who treated her in the same way mine had. The intelligence that I'd gathered on Faith before entering her family's home on the fateful night of our meeting had revealed no attempts to kidnap her and no attempts on her life up to that point.

"You still haven't answered the how," I said.

"You know how."

The Order of the Blood Moon had its own agenda—not that I'd been able to puzzle it out—and sometimes it took contracts when those contracts matched its aims. I never knew, going out on a job, whether the job originated internally or whether it'd been bought and paid for. I had my orders, and I followed them.

Some jobs stood out in my mind, and some faded into the blur of years and blood. The night I'd met Faith had been branded into my memory.

I could still smell the roses that had grown into hedges in front of her family's cookie-cutter, brick suburban home, thick and sultry in the humid air. The windows were dark. The wind gusted, rattling the trees of the live oak in the center of the front yard, the leaves whispering to one another. A storm was on the way, dark clouds jamming the horizon, lightning flashing far away, thunder rolling low and throaty. I caught the scent of rain, breathing it in deep, like a blessing. A hush consumed the whole neighborhood. How else could it be at 3:00 a.m.?

Even in the middle of the night, the air held on to a good portion of the day's heat. It seeped from the concrete, from the hard-baked earth. A black SUV crouched in the driveway like a guard dog that'd forgotten its duty and fallen asleep, its dark, tinted eyes tightly closed. If I needed to, I could use the SUV as a getaway vehicle. I shouldn't need to, though. Everything was going down as planned.

I went around the side of the house, opening the wooden gate with no trouble. They didn't bother locking the thing. The neighborhood was safe and if someone had wanted to get into the yard badly enough, they'd just hop the fence anyway. Sound reasoning.

A tall sycamore shaded the grass and the concrete patio, the grill and the water hose coiled like a serpent at its feet. Unlike the gate, the back door was locked, but if someone wanted to enter badly enough, they'd just pick the lock anyway. Silent as a mouse.

The door opened into a den. There was no art on the paneled pine walls except a velvet painting of the King of Rock 'n' Roll. An oversized sofa cut across the center of the room. A big-screen TV hugged the wall, a low bookcase beneath it serving as storage for game consoles and controllers. A stack of boxed board games sat in the corner.

Outside, the lightning flashed closer, thunder rumbling. The patter of rain on the roof and windows filled the room. Soon the gentleness of the water falling from the sky would give way to fury. The clouds had been too dark for anything less.

I waited. No use moving while the storm settled in. Better to wait a few minutes in case it caused my prey to wake, to give them the time to fall back to dreaming peacefully. That would make my job much easier on me—and them. I drew the gun strapped to my leg and screwed on the silencer. The gun was my backup weapon. I hated to use it, but it'd saved my life more than once. The weight of it grew heavier and more solemn with every minute I waited to move.

When I did finally weave a path through the kitchen with its black cat clock over the stove ticking away like a heartbeat and its breadcrumb-littered countertops and rag rug–covered linoleum floors, I heard the house sigh around me. Or perhaps I only felt it: my first inkling that something here wasn't as it seemed.

I headed down the adjacent hall, the floor carpeted now in plush beige, the walls lined with family photos—or, rather, photos of Faith's parents, and none of Faith herself. I passed a bathroom with a glowing purple butterfly night-light and a set of louvered doors that denoted a closet or a laundry room before coming to a stop in the open doorway of the master bedroom, where Faith's parents slept in king-sized comfort, their chests rising and falling in the slow, deep rhythm of people oblivious to the predator in their midst. Their halos were muted gold.

There was something else about them, though. Something I couldn't put my finger on. A quality to the color, maybe, that disturbed me on a primal level. I studied the scene.

Shed blue jeans and T-shirts and flip-flops lay in a pile at the foot of the bed, to one side of a laundry basket half full of dirty clothes. A painting of Our Lady of Guadalupe hung on the wall over the headboard, her bright colors muted in the dark, though I could still make out the iconography—she was bathed in golden rays of light, cloaked in starlit blue, lifted by the archangel Gabriel. Blinds covered the single window on the far wall, muted flashes seeping in along the sides when lightning arced across the sky. The faces of my prey remained smooth, untroubled.

I activated my magic with a single breath, my exhale longer than the inhale, slowing my heartbeat and shifting my consciousness and focusing on the woman. Instead of seeing her outside—her dusky skin, the thin white straps of the camisole she wore, the mussed brown hair that crowned her head—I slipped inside her dreaming mind.

She was younger than she was now in the dream, maybe twenty. She stood alone on the beach, not another human being in sight. Who came down to the beach in February? No one, really. It was too early. Too chilly. Maria—her name was Maria—had the whole place to herself. She was its queen.

Behind her, up the concrete stairs and over the seawall, another world was in motion. Cars passed on the main drag, their headlights sweeping. Streetlamps winked on. People gathered in restaurants and bars, knocking back drinks, bellies rumbling. For her, it was dark out, the fiery ball of the sun having just fallen below the waves. She'd watched it set, its reflection on the smoother water further out, her bare feet sunk into wet, shell-dotted sand. She curled her toes, enjoying the gentle sucking sensation as the sand gave way.

She breathed in the briny air, tasting the stink of seaweed on the back of her tongue, and closed her eyes as the wind gusted, whipping through her waist-length hair and the cornflower blue sweater and the bell-bottoms of her jeans and the hood of the white coat she wore, her gloved hands shoved in its pockets.

Her life was simple. She hadn't yet met Stuart, whom she would marry. She hadn't yet given birth to Faith. Maria never thought about having kids, in fact. She never thought she'd live a nightmare like the one she'd been drawn into.

Maria pushed the thought away. She stayed with the peace of the blustery night, the gentle whoosh and crash of the waves as they rolled in, the stars beginning to slink into the black velvet overhead.

It was a simple, peaceful matter to induce her to walk toward the water. The waves were icy at first, sending a shiver to the crown of Maria's head, to the core of her being. The next step, however, seemed warmer, and the next almost balmy.

Maria walked into the waves, pushing gently against their force and momentum, until the water brushed against her knees. And then her hips. And her shoulders. She walked until the water lifted her feet off the sandy bottom.

She sank underneath the surface, bubbles surfacing as she exhaled. When she breathed in again, she breathed in water rather than air. She kept walking, legs spinning in slow motion, as she drowned in her dream, simply and peacefully. Her body and mind, believing she was dead, gave up the ghost.

In the king-size bed beneath the painting of Our Lady of Guadalupe, her chest fell and did not rise.

I waited to confirm. Seconds ticked past. Maria didn't breathe again.

I turned my attention to her husband, Stuart—who was no longer asleep. Somehow, he'd sensed that something was wrong, that something bad had happened to his wife. His eyes snapped open, the whites of them too bright in the dark. And then I understood: he had magic of his own. That was how he had known, though not in time to save Maria.

He leapt from the bed and rushed me. I tried to slide into his mind, but whatever power he had held me at bay. I shot him in the chest. He went down like a sack of potatoes on top of the dirty laundry.

I stepped to him and hunkered down beside him, clapping my hand over his mouth and nose. He met my gaze and held it as his life slipped away, the bright whites of his eyes fading along with his consciousness.

Two down, one to go.

I pushed to my feet and went to the end of the hall, the carpet cushioning my step. I climbed the stairs slow and steady, careful to keep to the outside of the risers to avoid creaks. There were two rooms on the second floor. A game room, which was empty—and I mean empty, as in not a speck of furniture or art. And the child's bedroom with an en suite bathroom.

The bedroom was locked from the outside. Three deadbolts.

What the hell had Stuart and Maria done to the girl—to Faith? Why was the girl locked away? Why had the Order sent me here to kill them, with orders to kill their child as well?

No reason to kill a child unless the child witnessed a hit. Or unless the child was the target.

I'd considered those questions when I'd been given the assignment the prior morning. I'd felt a deep unease, but I hadn't dwelled on it until this moment. There hadn't been time. Besides, the Order had given me a place to be when no one else would have me, when I'd had nowhere else to go. They'd given me a place where I belonged. I was good at the work. I understood what the Order wanted—to consolidate its power.

To what end could a child possibly derail that goal? There were many ways to get to a child, not the least of which was to turn that child to the Order's own ends, to bring that child into the fold.

If the Order hadn't assigned this killing of its own volition, someone had hired the job done.

Someone. Or a group of someones.

Who would do such a thing? What kind of organization would approve of it? If I didn't want to be part of it anymore, if I wanted something else for my life, where could I go? Leaving was impossible. Wasn't it?

I shook my head to clear it, the memory of that night dissolving, the spicy scent of the *posole* and Jess's aunt Addie's face taking its place.

I held her gaze. "The Watchers hired the job that night, didn't they?"

Addie nodded. "At the time, we thought that Faith would be our enemy. We thought she would come down squarely on the side of an organization like the Order—or worse, on the side of those who are fomenting the apocalypse. It was thought that the best thing to do was to take her out of the equation. Nip all of the terrible possibilities in the bud."

"She was a child."

"So were you," Addie said.

"She was innocent."

"No one born with magic is innocent. We're born to choose. Good or evil. If you don't decide, you're choosing the bad guys by default. You ought to know, Night. You might've been a sweet little thing once upon a time, but your parents saw to it that whatever trust you had in the world, in people, was burnt to the ground along with their little frame house."

I remembered the fire. The way the burning had smelled—like the campfire my father had built in the backyard before he decided I was the Devil, the one we'd sat around and toasted marshmallows for s'mores over—only punctuated with the stench of melting plastic and sheetrock and furniture and human flesh.

My parents had burned in that fire.

"I'm not that little girl anymore," I said. "Why order the hit to include Faith's parents?"

"No loose ends," she said.

"That's way colder than I expect from someone who considers themselves one of the good guys."

"They knew what she was. If the wrong person came along and

asked the right questions, knowing what Faith was, they could bring her back," Addie said.

"Back to life?"

She nodded.

"Who could do that?" I didn't know of anyone who could do such a thing.

"There are a handful of magical beings who could do it," she said. "We couldn't take the chance."

"Name one," I said.

Addie pursed her lips. "The Angel of Death."

"I thought he was here because of me."

She held my gaze and said nothing.

"You don't know which of us the Angel is after," I said. "I'm just convenient to hang him on because you want me gone anyway."

She folded her arms across her chest.

"Goddamn you," I said.

She answered quietly, "Already happened a long time ago."

"Don't feel sorry for yourself about it," I said. "We've got more pressing things to worry about right now. For instance, are you aware that the kids are working on tracking the Angel of Death?"

Addie's eyebrows climbed to her hairline.

"I'll take that as a no," I said. "So, Jess didn't tell you."

"If she had, I'd have tanned her hide."

"Faith has been using her magic to help with tracking. I haven't yet had a chance to ask her which god she's been talking to."

Addie blanched. "There's only one God."

"No," I said. "There's yours, who would prefer that human beings have no other gods before him, and then there's the rest of them. Very powerful ones, worshipped by whole cultures; less powerful ones, worshipped by smaller tribes; and the local gods who walk the earth in human form and set down roots. It's a wide world. You know any of the local gods here, Addie?"

She pressed her lips together until they disappeared, preparing to argue with me. Maybe she saw in my face that arguing would be futile.

"No," she said. "I don't."

"Hear tell of any of them?"

"No," she said.

I pushed. "Anyone else?"

"One," she said grudgingly. "There's the Awakened."

"Sounds like a god," I said.

She snorted. "Supposedly, he—she, it they, whatever—lurks inside someone in this city like a parasite, waiting for the right time to wake up and take over. The poor person doesn't even know there's something inside them. It's terrible. I couldn't imagine a more terrible thing to happen to a living, breathing human being than to have their agency taken away like that."

"That's all you know about it?"

"I've heard gossip about it only recently—the last few months. The thing is supposed to have infiltrated someone with magic already, so in addition to taking over that person's will, it'll have their magic to boot."

"Why?"

"Why what?" Addie asked.

"Why would a god need a human being like that?"

"Maybe it lost its own body a long time ago. Maybe it can't act here in this plane, this dimension, without a body—like the Angel. I don't know. The only other thing I've heard is that the Awakened is supposed to be showing up now because of the coming war. It's a player."

"Who'd you hear it from?" I asked.

"Hell, no," she said. "I'm not giving you a single name of anybody I know just so you can go torture and kill them for information."

"If I was going to torture and kill someone, I could've started with you," I said.

"We have a deal. Guest rights."

"Which, if I was as awful as you say I am, I'd have agreed to and then broken as soon as I didn't feel like keeping my worthless word." I stood up. "I'm gonna work the Angel of Death angle with Faith and see if I can get out of her and her friends exactly what they've done so far and how close they've gotten. I might get distracted if the Order shows, since odds are they've found us or will any minute, so we'll see how far I get. I'll report back to you what I find. In return, you rescind whatever hit you put out on me."

"We didn't do that," she said.

"No?"

"I planned to do my own killing this time."

"While I'm a guest in your home," I said. "Yeah, who's the monster again?"

She had the good grace to flush with shame. "I'll talk with Jess."

"Great idea. Let me know what she tells you."

Addie signed. "There are a lot of moving parts here, Night."

"Too many. We have to start somewhere."

"We," she said.

"Never thought you'd work with a reformed killer, did you?"

"If I don't? If I stick to the plan as it stood before you rang my doorbell?"

"I'll kill you," I said. "I won't want to. And you might beat the hell out of me physically or magically, but you won't stop me. You don't stand a chance. I'm better at it than you. I have a lot more practice. And I'll be doing it to protect me and mine, not some ideal—I'm not out to save the world, Addie. Don't cross me."

She mulled over my words. After a moment, she pulled a phone from her back pocket. "What's your number?"

I gave it to her. A few seconds later, my phone buzzed with an incoming text.

"Now you have mine," she said. "Let me know what you find. I'll work on Jess separately and do the same."

"So we have a deal?" I asked.

"We have a truce. Temporarily."

"Think carefully before you break it," I said.

I walked out of the kitchen, with all the memories it stirred, slipped on my sneakers, and stepped out of her house into the misty world. I zipped my hoodie and drew the hood into place, the perfume of lavender and rosemary filling my nose and mouth with every breath. Fine drops of moisture collected on my clothes and skin as I made my way down the steps to my car. I sat inside for a good minute, my heart beating a little too fast and my breath fogging the windshield.

I'd meant every single world I'd said to Addie. I would kill her if I had to. The fact that I wasn't an Order operative anymore didn't matter at all. My regrets didn't count on that score either. Faith did.

I turned over the rest of Addie's and my conversation in my mind, examining all its facets like a jeweler would a diamond's, and comparing it with what Sunday had told me. My thoughts came to rest on the end of everything as I understood it: Watchers. The Angel of Death. The gathering of powers and the choosing of sides.

The world had come close to ending before. Disaster had been averted. Was this time different? Could the apocalypse be stopped? If not, could its trajectory be altered?

Could a single person even begin to try?

It seemed worth trying. The one thing I couldn't abide was the idea of inevitability, of a fate that couldn't be changed, that my choices didn't matter. It might've felt true that, for a great part of my life, I'd had no choice about what I'd become and what I'd done. But I knew better now. I refused to pretend otherwise.

The ringing of harp strings filled the car. It took me a second to understand that the sound came from my phone and to dig the thing out of my pocket. I saw Red's number on the caller ID.

He'd want answers. What could I possibly tell him?

I answered the call just before it went to voice mail.

Red's voice filled my ear, too loud, too frantic.

"Wait," I said. "What? Slow down."

"Faith's gone," he said. "She must've slipped out while I was in the back."

She could've sneaked out while Red wasn't looking. Or Jess could've circled back around for her on Watcher business, implementing a plan to get Faith away from me with or without her aunt's approval. Or Sunday could've taken Faith. Or someone with the Order. Or the Angel of Freaking Death.

Red had her number, and she had his, just in case there was any kind of problem. He was the only person in the city I really knew. I asked him the next logical question despite already knowing the answer. "Did you try to call her?"

"Yeah," he said. "She didn't pick up. Didn't answer a text either."

I sucked in a breath. "I'll be right there."

"No," he said. "If you know where she might have gone, I'll meet you there."

I focused down, clearing my thoughts. "The place where Faith went last night. Ben's house."

"See you in ten," Red said, and hung up.

I pulled away from the curb, tires skidding and sliding before they caught traction, leaving rubber on the road.

CHAPTER 5

I PULLED TO A SCREECHING STOP behind Red's dark blue Ford pickup. He'd parked along the right-side curb in front of Ben's house and leaned against the driver's side door in the mist, hands shoved into the pockets of a black jean jacket that he'd shrugged on over his hoodie. His halo shone grass green and dark earth colors, but darker than usual from worry. He opened my door as I cut the engine. I stepped out to join him, the chill seeping straight through my clothes and into my bones.

The street was supernaturally quiet except for the thin sound of the falling mist and the slow tick of the Honda's engine. To our left, a neighborhood park filled with play equipment sat lonely and vacant, except for a single crow that had taken up residence on the rail at the top of the slide. The trees that lined the street were all maples except the one in front of Ben's place, which was a hawthorn. When it bloomed, it would flower white, with red berries dripping from its thorny branches. Now its form was hollowed out by the season, but it was still a powerful being with the purpose of guarding the house, just like Addie's lavender and rosemary. It had a halo that resembled is magical form—an impenetrable hedge.

The hawthorn was actively on guard, but did not seem overly interested in us.

I led the way up the walk to the house, my sneakers sliding on wet, packed leaves that'd drifted into the yard and slicked the driveway, where Ben's father's gray Fiat crouched, while Red dogged my heels. The place was a gray duplex, and Ben and his dad had the left side. I took the two steps to the porch in one bound and knocked loudly since there was no bell.

Ben answered the door. He'd changed from his gym clothes into dark jeans and a long-sleeved, black T-shirt. He'd thrown a gray tee that matched his gray halo over the top. He shook the long bangs to one side, giving me a great view of one of his brown eyes. He stretched his arms above his head, leaning forward to grip the doorjamb and effectively blocking the entry.

"Night," he said. "You're looking for Faith again, right?"

I held his gaze. "We know she's here."

"Yeah," he said. "Where else would she be?"

Red moved to stand beside me. "At the gym, with me. That's where she should be. And you should be at school."

"We had something more important to do, so we skipped out," Ben said.

"You want to step out of the way?" Red asked.

"Not really," Ben said. "Like I said, we're doing something important right now and we need—" he pushed up his sleeve to reveal a silver watch on a black leather band, and checked the time "—another twenty seconds."

I pushed into the doorway, forcing him back.

He hadn't expected that. He backpedaled to avoid being knocked on his ass, but he maneuvered to a stop in front of me, reaching out with his left hand to grab the edge of a table—maple legs, granite top. It held a brass bowl for keys and a stack of bills still in their white envelopes. On the far side of the table, a coat rack held a colorful mountain of fleece and down coats. Ben's white ten-speed bike leaned against the wall, a white helmet perched on top of the seat.

The stairs were behind him. He looked at them in panic. Faith—and the important work—must be happening on the second floor.

He noticed that I noticed. "Wait," he said.

I leaned in with my shoulder and he moved again, falling into the table, scattering envelopes to the floor.

I took the wooden steps two at a time, up the first flight and onto the landing, pivoting left and up the second flight. Behind me, Ben and Red pushed and shoved, scrambling up the steps. I didn't look back, only forward. Beads of sweat popped at the small of my back. The heat in the house had been turned up. It wrapped me in suffocating arms.

There was an open space with a window that showed a view of the park and a plant stand beneath it filled with small clay pots of herbs, some for cooking, some for magic. To the left, a bathroom still steamy from someone's shower. To the right, Ben's bedroom. The door was closed. The narrow space between the bottom of the door and the floor leaked thick, resiny smoke that reeked of patchouli.

A hand grabbed a fistful of my hoodie from behind. Ben's.

"Wait another second," he said.

I slapped his hand away and opened the door to his room, eyes stinging from the incense smoke. An altar had been set up in the center of the room on a black cloth—a grouping of six white seven-day candles in glass jars, wicks burning merrily, and one black candle with its flame snuffed. The altar included the incense burner, too, still smoking, and a single Tarot card with the image of the Grim Reaper swinging his scythe: Death.

Three surprised faces stared at me, wide eyes and open mouths and palpable relief. Whatever they'd been doing, they'd barely finished. Ben had managed to delay me just enough.

Faith sat on the floor in front of the altar, a shine of perspiration on her forehead, her dark eyes not quite focused. She'd stripped off her sweater, and the white camisole she'd worn underneath it was damp with sweat, too. The heat came from inside her. Warm as she appeared at first glance, goose bumps laced her arms. She looked at me with a combination of gratitude and terror.

I tore my gaze away from hers to give the side-eye to Corey and Jess.

Corey sat cross-legged in the seat of the swivel chair at Ben's glass-and-steel desk on the far side of the room, underneath a window that hid behind a pull-down, khaki blackout shade. She was dressed in the same skeletal cameo jewelry and dark blue, pleated plaid dress with matching tights that she had been wearing this morning, though she'd kicked off her boots.

On the west side of the room, Jess perched on the edge of Ben's impeccably made bed crowned with a white down comforter. Her short, muscled frame was wrapped in a duster-length, chocolate-brown sweater with big, speckled matching buttons. She wore plum-colored cords and matching toe socks. There was another window right behind her, guarded by a second blackout shade.

She narrowed her eyes, taking in parts of me that could only be seen by the magical eye. "You went to my house, talked with my aunt," she said. "I can see her all over you. She made you a promise."

"We're working together for now," I said.

She shook her head, the ghost of a grin taking over her mouth. "Don't know how you managed that, but it's a load off my conscience."

I was in no mood to talk about anything except what I'd narrowly missed. "What have y'all been doing in here?"

Ben stepped into the room, weaving a path around me, coming to stand near the bed, closest to Jess. "I asked you to wait."

"You tried to keep me from my kid," I said. "I need an answer to my question."

The three of them glanced at each other, heaping the spokesperson job on Ben.

"Summoning," he said, finally.

A finger of fear touched my heart. "Summoning who?"

"Whom," he said.

"Not in the mood for grammar games, Ben."

"Him," he said. "The Angel."

I kept my voice even, although I felt anything but even inside. "Why in holy hell would you do such a thing?"

"According to Jess, he's coming anyway," Ben said.

"So you figured, why wait?"

He shrugged. "We had some questions for him."

Questions? "What could you possibly ask him before he turns all of you to dust or worse? Not that I know what the Angel of Death would do to a bunch of kids who had the balls to summon him for an interrogation session."

"We can protect ourselves," Ben said.

I shook my head. "You have no idea what you're getting into."

"Neither do you, Night," he said.

"You're right," I said. "The difference is, I have a healthy amount of respect for things I don't understand."

He came back quickly. "Fear's not the same thing as respect."

I held his gaze. "Fear is a normal, sane response to beings who are higher on the food chain than you. For instance, sharks, tigers, and angels who kick off the end of the world."

Ben opened his mouth to respond, but Faith interrupted. "Ben's covering for me."

We turned to look at her.

"It's not covering," Ben said. "We have your back."

Faith had smudges beneath her eyes—not black eyes, and not quite the luggage usually acquired through lack of sleep. She'd not only used her power, she'd over-used it. Her halo had reverted to its usual color since this morning, though it still held a hint of the spark and flame with which she'd marched into the gym. Instead of shimmering, though, her halo had a dull edge to it, as if the glow had been rubbed off.

I squatted down to be on her level, to look her in the eye. "This summoning was your idea?"

She nodded. "After what Jess said outside the gym this morning, I needed to know whether the Angel was coming here because of you—or me."

Jess drew her brows into a V. "Never said anything about this being your fault."

"Most of the bad things that happen are," Faith said. "Like my parents."

"You lived. They didn't. That doesn't make them dying your fault," Jess said.

Faith went on as if she hadn't heard Jess. "We have to watch our backs, and that's because of me. The couple of times I used my magic before we came here, I almost got us killed. Then I did it here, and we can't run now even if we wanted to because it won't matter. So if Death is coming for me and there's nothing I can do about it this time, I wanted to at least know why."

Jess bent forward, resting her elbows on her knees. "Still not your fault."

Faith looked at me—no, past me, over my shoulder. "What do you think, Red?"

He'd climbed the steps after me, and that meant he had to be behind me, listening. Paying quiet, focused attention.

Red had magic, and he used it to help the kids who found a way to his gym, but the kind of stuff we were talking about was way over his head. I glanced over my shoulder.

He leaned against the doorjamb, hands in the front pockets of his jeans. His face was a map of emotions: concern, sadness, care. I didn't read any fear there, nor did it show in his halo. "I have a lot of questions myself," he said. "Mostly what I want to know right now is whether the summoning worked."

Corey swiveled in the desk chair to face him. "I believe it did, just not the way we planned."

"What's that mean, exactly?" Red asked.

Corey tucked her hair behind her ears, her cheeks flushing nearly as red as her locks. "We thought we were bringing him here, but he didn't show. Normally, that would mean what we tried didn't work."

"You've got experience in that department?" Red asked.

"You don't learn anything new if you don't try," she said.

Red pushed off the wall and took a step into the room. "But?"

"But the black candle went out. That was supposed to be our clue that the summoning had worked. The candle would go out and then the Angel would appear."

"We got one, but not the other," Faith said.

"You did the summoning wrong," Red said.

Corey sighed. "Or we did it right and we summoned the Angel, but he decided to show up close by instead of in this room."

I looked at Corey. "How close?"

"The radius of the summoning spell is ten miles," she said.

"Ten square miles," I said.

"Yes. Any direction from here."

I shook my head. So much ground to cover—no, there was no use trying. "You expected the Angel to answer your questions and then what?"

"To do what Death does," Faith said.

"Kill you all, like I brought up with Ben before?"

"No," Faith said. "Just me."

I cocked my head. "You were willing to sacrifice yourself?"

She nodded.

Ben's hands curled into fists. "Hell, no."

Clearly Faith hadn't shared her plan with her friends, and they hadn't thought things through enough to know there'd be a price at the end of the game.

I held up a hand. "Did any of you know that the Angel of Death doesn't have his own body? That he has to possess a body in order to act here in this world?"

For imparting this revelation, I received four looks filled with horror and a lot of stunned silence.

Faith slowly pushed to her feet. "You're telling us that if we successfully summoned the Angel, he's busy possessing some poor unsuspecting bastard, somewhere out there?"

I nodded. "Most people don't like that too much. Most people fight it. It may take a while for the Angel to take complete control."

"How long?" Faith asked.

"Usually a day, maybe a little bit less."

"How do you know all of this?" Ben asked.

"I studied." I'd done the kind of investigating I imagine anyone who'd had an attempted exorcism performed on them might do. I'd tried to understand. Of course, the Order had more complete, available information on possession than I was ever likely to squeeze out of a priest.

"You're right," Faith said. "We're in over our heads."

Ben tensed up even further, but he kept his lip zipped.

"We need help," Faith said.

"All right," I said. I'd be whatever help I could, and I had no doubt that Red would do the same, and Addie, too. But would we be enough?

"What should we do?" Corey asked.

"We stay here and pool information," I said. "Y'all have been working on this for a while, and I need to know what you do. I've talked to Jess's aunt, and I have a bit of information she told me, but it might be best to have her here."

Jess pulled out her phone and dialed, moving from the bed out into the open area outside the room.

"Corey and Ben, can y'all order pizzas? Something to eat, some drinks. We're gonna need all the sustenance we can get right now."

Corey nodded and walked out, but Ben stayed behind. His halo darkened to the gray that reminded me of the Texas sky, holding its breath before a thunderstorm.

"Why are you helping?" he asked.

From the set of his shoulders, which were busy climbing toward his ears, he wasn't really curious about the food. Or why I was helping, which should've been easy to see.

"I'm not trying to take over here," I said.

Red stepped between Ben and me. "Why not?" he asked.

It seemed like the obvious question. Red and I were the adults here. Adults being in charge was the normal thing to expect, the thing to do. "Because we all need to be on the same page or this isn't gonna work. I don't want anyone pissed off, rolling on their own. That's how people get hurt. That's how they get dead."

Red took a deep breath and blew it out slowly. "Okay."

I raised a brow at Ben. He didn't seem one-hundred-percent convinced. "I have a lot more experience in this area than you," I said.

"Summoning angels or fighting them?" he asked.

"Neither," I said. "Going into deadly situations and fighting my way out of them? Yes. Using my magic offensively and making it work when everything is on the line? That, too."

He blinked at me. "You're a gym coach."

"No," I said. "Well, yes, for the last few months, but before that, no."

"What are you, then?" he asked.

"I'd tell you, but then I'd have to kill you," I said.

He laughed, but the laughter faded when I didn't join him. "You were kidding."

"Better you don't know." If he knew who I was, what I was, then he'd become someone the Order could use to help find me and Faith.

I showed him a rueful grin. I couldn't help noting the irony in the words that had just rolled off my tongue given what I'd said to Addie about tying up loose ends, about how cold it was to have included Faith's folks in the hit she ordered only for that reason. The truth was, I understood exactly where she was coming from. I just didn't claim to be on the side of the angels like she did.

How many jobs had the Order sent me on with multiple targets? More than I could count on two hands. How many of those were like my last job, where one person was the target and everyone else amounted to collateral damage—tying up loose ends? No witnesses, no problems after the fact.

But there was always fallout, whether it was among any remaining loved ones of the people I'd taken out or in my own heart. What about the children who might grow up without their parents? Or the husband or wife or lover who would never be the same again? What about the important things my targets had begun that they would never finish? Or vital things they would have done that they'd never get a chance to start? When did it end?

It didn't. It couldn't.

Ben shook his head. "That's not going to work for me, Night. Two minutes ago, you said that we had to pool information, share everything we know. You said you weren't trying to take charge. You want us to be in this together. And now you're doing the opposite of that. Now you're keeping secrets."

I looked at Red, hoping that he'd back me up. He met my gaze, but didn't say a word.

I closed my eyes. I had no right to expect anything from Red. After all, I'd lied to him about who I was, and he knew it. Keeping the pertinent details of my past from Ben and the others might keep Faith and me safe—whatever that meant with several flavors of hell bearing down on us—but it wouldn't do the same for the rest of us. In fact, not knowing about Sunday—about the Order—could put them in serious danger. It could very well get them killed. They would be a very different kind of loose end: the kind who ended up exploited, the kind who ended up sacrificed without even knowing why.

"You won't like it," I said.

"Good," Ben said. "I mean, good if it means you're some kind of ninja. You pushed me out of the way downstairs."

"That was nothing. And if you don't want to be pushed out of the way, you need to learn to stand your ground."

"You're a girl. I didn't want to hit you."

"You don't have to use your fists," I said. "And you're gonna have to get over the girl thing. That rule is great for regular interactions, for relationships. It doesn't work so well if someone who means you harm is coming after you. Ninjas aren't gonna be impressed by your chivalry. They're gonna break your neck."

He stared at me.

I smiled at him again, this time gently. "Go help Corey. I'll talk while we eat."

A visible weight lifted from him, his halo lightening three shades. He did what I asked.

I let go of a breath I hadn't realized I'd been holding. I turned my focus to Faith. "We should talk, too," I said. "Just the two of us."

She nodded. "Can we do that a little later? I feel like I'm gonna throw up."

That made two of us. "Sure."

"You're not mad?" she asked.

"I'm definitely mad, but mostly I'm glad you're okay."

"Am I grounded?"

What a question. "I think we're past that, Faith."

"Just don't leave me," she said. "Or make me leave."

I took her hands in mine. "Not gonna happen."

She wiped her forehead—and her eyes—with her sleeve. I pretended not to notice.

"Are you really gonna tell them all of that?" she asked. "About your magic?"

"I think I have to," I said. "But I'm not gonna tell them anything about you. You want to do that, it's up to you."

"Now I really think I'm gonna throw up," she said.

That made two of us. If I told everyone about my magic, there would be questions about the ways in which I'd used it, how I'd honed my skills, where I'd received my training. Those were things no one in this house knew except me. Things I'd never told Faith because to tell her meant that she would know for certain, if she hadn't already guessed, how I came to be in her family's home the night her parents died.

"I'd like to step outside. Get a little fresh air," I said.

"Backyard's good for that," she said. "I'll go with them."

Meaning her friends. "Stay with them. No taking off this time."

She nodded.

I turned to go.

Red tracked with me. "Keep you company."

It wasn't an offer that could be declined.

Our walk through the house was a blur. I noticed some things—my training wouldn't allow me to shut down completely regardless of whether fear for Faith and the others threatened to take me to my knees, or whether I was about to have a dreaded conversation with Red that I'd known would come eventually if I stayed in Portland long enough, just not like this. We walked downstairs again and down the long hall past the living room, where I caught a glimpse of an overstuffed, brown leather sofa and a long, leather-wrapped coffee table around which the kids had congregated while Ben hunkered down in front of the hearth, building a fire, and through the kitchen, which smelled richly of dark roasted coffee. We passed through the laundry room, which held a huge plastic basket overflowing with dirty clothes, then out the door onto an indoor/outdoor porch.

There was a roof over our heads, a circle of painted, white wooden chairs with dark green outdoor cushions on which to sit, and an unlit, blackened woodstove in the center of the circle. The porch looked out onto a mostly fallow garden, but part of the plot held winter greens that grew strong. A windowless, wooden shed with an aluminum roof crouched in the very back of the yard. Droplets of mist covered it all. Mist hung in the air, too, as if it were suspended and time itself had stopped.

What I wouldn't give for that to happen, even if I could have only a few minutes to clear my head, to think.

It wasn't to be. The mist gathered on the roof of the porch and dripped from the eaves, reminding me that time moved on. It always had.

My legs trembled—maybe a little from the cold, but mostly from the avalanche of doom that had started before dawn and continued to fall. I sat in the nearest chair with a view of the garden, squeezing a whistle of air from the cushion as my weight settled.

Red shoved the chair beside mine as close as he could get it, then sat on the edge of the seat. He leaned forward, resting his head in his hands. When he glanced up again—at the yard and then at me—he reached for my hand. I let him take it and hold it in both of his. They were warm. I hadn't realized my hands were cold.

"There's some things I need to tell you," he said.

CHAPTER 6

THE PORCH FELT COLDER, the water that dripped from the eaves striking the edge of the floor and the earth sharply, like knives. The mouth of the woodstove looked like a door to hell. The mist seemed to obscure the garden and the wooden shed in the back of the yard, closing us off from the world. There was only Red and me and whatever secret he'd harbored.

He wasn't the one who was supposed to be hiding things from me. It was supposed to be the other way around.

He avoided my gaze, looking down at his hands and my hand sandwiched in between. His silver hair fell across his face. "I was waiting for the right time to say all this, but it never came."

"Maybe now is the right time," I said.

"The only time, Night."

"Okay," I said. "Spell it out, whatever it is."

"You were expecting demands," he said. "Why'd you lie to me, who are you really, what in God's name is going on—all that?"

I nodded.

"I do have those questions, and I'm gonna need answers, but you're not the only one who's been holding out, and my secrets are as old as yours."

I'd never really wondered. I mean, I'd considered why he hadn't asked more questions when he hired me, and the level of trust in me his actions showed, but I hadn't wanted to look the proverbial gift horse in the mouth. I hadn't wanted to ruin a good thing, not when I finally felt like I had something to lose.

"I didn't recognize you at first," he said.

Recognize me? I narrowed my eyes at him. How could he know me when I hadn't known him until I'd walked through the door of his gym?

He went on. "I mean, I thought you were something special because of what you said, and because of how you were with the kids who came into the gym, and then when I met Faith, I was impressed with how you were with her. You were so closed-mouthed about your past. I could respect that. And then about two weeks after you started, when you were extra tired, you laid down on the floor in my office to catch some shut-eye. Just a nap."

I'd only done that the once. I'd been up all night with Faith. She'd had a hard time adjusting, and she felt sick. She hadn't wanted to talk about it, so we'd just snuggled on the sofa and watched movies until just before dawn. The next day, she hung out at the gym with me in the morning. She'd met Jess, made a friend. They'd gone to get coffee and I'd sacked out for a twenty-minute power nap.

"What about it?" I asked.

"The way you slept, the way you looked, reminded me of someone I'd known a long time ago. I did some digging."

"There's nothing to dig into," I said. I'd been very careful in constructing my identity. I had no past to discover, as far as the rest of the world was concerned. No one would be able to find anything on me that I didn't want found, and I'd never reveal a thing. At least, that'd been the case until today.

"I noticed," he said. "But my research isn't—wasn't—confined to normal channels."

Normal channels. Mundane, everyday channels. "Magic."

He nodded.

"You see the good in people when others don't," I said.

"Reading my halo?"

I blinked at him.

"Thought so."

"How'd you know?" Knowing the flavor of other people's magic wasn't something that most people had the aptitude for.

"I see into people, Night. More than the good. Also the bad, the ugly, and the unspeakable. Usually, my view is pretty surface-level, but I can go deeper if I want or need to. I can catch a glimpse of someone's soul. I'd seen yours before."

The intimacy of what he said, and the plain way he said it, made me want to pull my hand from his. I tugged, but he refused to let go.

"We're from the same place," he said.

A place I never wanted to go again. A city I still saw in my nightmares. "Houston."

"You spent two nights and a day at my house."

I shook my head. "I'd remember that. I'd remember you."

"You were twelve," he said.

I'd left the city at that age. The Order had taken me.

"Your house was burning," he said. "I hid you in my closet that night and most of the next. I kept you safe."

I sucked in a breath.

Just a few hours ago, Addie had brought up that night. I'd told her I wasn't that girl any longer. I'd meant it.

But in this moment, it wasn't quite true. If I closed my eyes, I could feel the heat on my skin and smell the stink of my own singed hair, the ends brittle and broken off in the dark confines of a long, narrow place—a closet—occupied by myself and two others.

A boy with dark red hair that stuck up where he'd slept on it—he was one. He spoke with a subtle Southern drawl and wore a black T-shirt with the sleeves cut off and a hastily donned pair of jeans creased at the seams from ironing. He wore scuffed white sneakers without socks. There'd been no time for socks. There'd been no time for anything except doing.

He'd grabbed me around the waist as I slinked through his backyard, clapping a hand over my mouth so that I wouldn't call out—not that I'd have so much as whimpered. I didn't have it in me. I wanted only to disappear. I had nothing left inside—no feeling, no fight. If he'd tried to hurt me, I don't know whether I'd have had it in me to struggle against him. He was strong, his grip like iron. I was small and wiry and weak. He hadn't hurt me.

His halo was colored with green and earth-brown. Solid. Steady. Safe.

He spoke low in my ear, the minty scent of toothpaste on his breath, about cops and the fire department on the way, and I believed him because I could hear the sirens. He said bad people were in the neighborhood. That they'd search for me. If I didn't hide, maybe they'd find me. I believed that, too, because it rang true in the depths of my bones, so I went inside with him.

He settled me in the dark, carpeted closet in his room with a pillow and a sheet and a guard—a blond Lab so old that her muzzle had gone completely gray. He said her name was Dorothy, like from *The Wizard of Oz*. I wrapped my arms around her and breathed in the heady perfume of grass and dirt and oatmeal shampoo. Dorothy let me do that. She rested her head on my shoulder.

The clothes hanging on the overhead rack made the space seem smaller, more secure. Shoes had been pushed into the far corner, but the sweaty-feet smell wafted along the floor and clung to the carpet.

After a while—after the law and the firefighters arrived, sirens cut off, red-and-blue lights still flashing—they shone in through the boy's bedroom window and through the crack in the center of the closet's double doors—sleep swallowed me whole. I didn't wake up when Red crawled into the closet and closed the door behind him, or when the fire was finally snuffed out, or when the sun poked its head over the horizon. I slept through the whole day.

I know this only because Red told me when I finally did wake. He said nothing about the bad people, and I was afraid to ask.

He brought me some leftovers from dinner that he said was macaroni and cheese, but it tasted like ashes in my mouth. My hair stuck to my face, damp with sweat, and reeked of smoke, as did my pink T-shirt and soot-stained white shorts. I sat up in the closet and pushed myself back against the wall, drawing my knees in close.

Red asked questions. I tried to answer them, but when I opened my mouth, nothing came out. The emptiness that I'd felt before I'd fallen asleep had gone. In its place, I felt like a hollowed-out stone into which every awful feeling in the whole world poured itself like poisoned water. Rage and terror and grief. My eyes filled with water, but no tears fell.

Red said I should sleep some more. He said he knew what I had done and he didn't blame me. He said that in the morning, we would figure out what to do.

I think he meant to stay up all night, watching over me, but eventually his eyes fluttered closed. Maybe he'd stayed up all the night before, and two nights wide awake was too many.

He knew what I had done and he didn't blame me.

How could he know when I didn't remember what had happened? I took his words in and imagined every possibility, zeroing in on the only possible conclusion: I'd killed my parents.

I shoved the thought away as though it burned me, like the fire had burned them.

I slipped out of the closet and out the bedroom window, scraping my leg on the sill. I had no idea where to go, just that I couldn't stay. I took one last look at my house next door, at the blackened beams and shattered glass, imagining all the memories inside that had burned up. The first good feeling pierced my heart: gratitude.

The smell, though—the horrible stench the flames had left behind—rushed into my nose and mouth. My stomach rolled over. I leaned forward, hands on my knees, and threw up what remained of the macaroni and cheese.

After that, I forced myself to take shallow breaths. I made myself look at Red's house, at the yard with a drainage ditch at the curb and scraggly grass, at an old, decrepit oak tree with an aching back bent over on the lawn. The little frame house had been painted bright blue with white once upon a time, but now the color had faded to barely there. A clay garden gnome lay on its side on the postage-stamp porch.

I'd seen Red a lot of times over the years, mostly by himself. His mother worked three jobs. I never saw her. Red worked after school, stocking grocery shelves. If he had a father, I'd never seen him. If Red's mother had come home while he'd been hiding me, I hadn't heard her. The thoughts jumbled in my head, not making sense.

For one crystal clear beat, though, I wondered whether Red really had anybody. Whether he was all alone.

The moment passed. The air was still and heavy and humid. It clung to my skin. I walked along the curb, walking in the opposite direction of the burnt husk that had been my house, focusing on keeping to the shadows so that no one would see me—the shadows of the houses, of the live oaks and pines in the yards, the shadows of the cars parked on the sides of the road. I stayed out of the puddled light of the street lamps.

I made it five blocks before the long, black car pulled up in front of me and the woman got out. She wore all black, like a mourner—even her hair. She smelled like ice and her halo was the color of liquid silver, her voice rhythmic like the song of cicadas. She said she'd come to help me. She said she knew I had magic, and that was all right with her.

She didn't feel safe like the boy had. She felt dangerous, but she seemed to be on my side. And I had nowhere else to go and no one to go to, and the bad people were still out there somewhere, so I went with her. The air conditioning in the car chilled the skin on my arms to gooseflesh. The leather seat stuck to the backs of my legs.

She'd taken me to the Order. She—

I breathed out a ragged breath.

The misty chill of Portland was a far cry from that sticky summer night in Texas. The boy who'd helped me had become the man who sat beside me now, though the halo looked and felt exactly the same. How could I not have recognized it the first time I walked into the gym? How could I not have recognized Red?

It'd been so long. A lifetime ago.

My voice shook as I started to speak, steadying as the words flowed. "What are the odds, Red? What are the odds that you and I would end up in the same place at the same time again?"

"Honestly, I don't know," he said. "Be nice to think it's a coincidence, but I don't believe in those."

"No one with magic believes in those."

"Like I said, I was planning to tell you as soon as I figured out the right time and the right way. I thought you'd be angry."

"Maybe I should be, but I have bigger, badder things to be pissed about right now, and you have my back."

He glanced away, scanning the garden. "I didn't follow you or track you down or anything like that. You disappeared from my life when you were twelve, and I had no way to find you. So if this isn't a coincidence, what's brought us back together?"

"Could be all the current threats," I said. "Or any single one of them."

"Could also be something else altogether."

"No way to know," I said. "Not yet, anyway."

He nodded. "So how much do you remember about that night?"

"Too much," I said, "and not enough. I blocked out most of it—everything that happened that night inside my house, with my parents. I remember being asleep, but not deeply. I hadn't been able to relax enough to sleep properly in a couple of weeks. I remember the sound of footsteps coming down the hall toward my room, and the creaking of the floorboards. That's it."

"Maybe that's a blessing."

I shook my head. "Just because I don't remember consciously doesn't mean that the memories aren't still in here somewhere. I need to know what really happened."

Red looked at me. "Why?"

"It haunts me. I have nightmares."

"What if knowing makes things worse?" he asked.

"Anything would be better than wondering."

"No," he said.

"I have a very good imagination and a lot of experience with a lot of very bad things, Red."

"So you keep saying."

I shifted in my seat, angling my body toward his. "What did you see in me that night?"

He squeezed my hand and mulled the question, taking his time with an answer. "It's not what I saw in you that night that mattered, it was what I saw before when I looked into you. The magic, sure—that was obvious. It was the way you were reluctant to use it because you were afraid of hurting anyone with it. There was a sweetness inside of you, an innocence, a sense of wonder. You had a good heart, Rose."

Rose. Rosa Guadalupe Jimenez Ruiz. The name my parents had given me the morning I was born.

"No one's called me that in a very long time."

"It doesn't fit anymore," he said.

"No, it doesn't." I breathed the cold air deep into my lungs. "You still haven't answered my question."

"Because it wasn't important," he said.

"It's important to me."

He swallowed hard. "The night your parents died, when I looked into you, I saw nothing at all. It was as if you—whoever you'd been before—were just gone. It was as if you'd become a blank slate. Then there was one small, hopeful thing—a barely-there spark that lit inside of you as the sun came up."

"Any idea what the spark was?"

"Maybe a will to live? Maybe something inside of you waking up for the first time," he said.

I didn't know what to think, or what to feel. The emptiness made sense, and the spark. Red's words flashed me back to this morning's talk with Addie, and what she said about the god known only as the Awakened, the god that dwelled inside a person of magical power, but remained dormant until one day it would come to life.

If it dwelled inside of me, if it had been the spark in me all those years ago, surely I would know by now.

"Red?"

He met my gaze.

"What do you see now?"

"It's part of why I didn't recognize you. It's different—not like either of the times I looked before." The corners of his mouth curved into a soft smile. "You're all sharp, steel edges, and the sweetness is nothing but a memory."

That hurt to hear, although it rang true deep. I curled my free hand into a loose fist, rubbing my knuckles over my heart.

"Sweetness is overrated," Red said. "You're different now because you're older, and you've been through a crucible—at least one. What you have now is kindness. That's valuable. That's everything."

I stared at him.

He rose from his seat and pulled me with him, letting go of my hand to gather me in his arms. I stiffened for a heartbeat—I couldn't remember the last time someone had held me. I'd done all the holding, all the comforting, all of my life.

I breathed in the green and earth of his halo, the faint scents of soap and tea tree shampoo, chill and rain that lingered on his skin and in his hair. His arms and chest were strong and hard with muscle, but he held me gently—not as if I might break, but as something, someone, cherished. I wrapped my arms around his waist and held on tight, taking what he offered and giving what I could.

The hum of an engine and the squeal of belts and brakes undercut the plip-plop of the water that dripped from the eaves. Someone had pulled into the driveway, and judging from the commotion inside the house, that someone carried an insulated bag filled with pizzas.

Moment of truth, and not just for fessing up to the group about who I was. The most important person in my entire world was in there, waiting to hear a story from me about who I used to be before I became her guardian. I could leave out plenty, and maybe I could skirt the parts I'd hidden from Faith, but all it would take was someone asking the wrong question, or putting the right details together at the wrong time, and my carefully built house of cards would come crashing down all around us. The only thing worse than Faith finding out what I'd done was her finding out from someone else.

Maybe she'd lose whatever trust she had in me. Maybe that could be rebuilt, or maybe it couldn't. Maybe she'd hate me. I could live with that if I had to. What I couldn't live with was her hating herself—that, I had no control over.

"We should go in," I said. "I'm gonna want a few minutes to talk with Faith before I talk with the rest of you."

"Something you need to tell her?" he asked.

"I've been keeping something from her. I don't think I can do that anymore. It might not go well."

He planted a soft kiss on my forehead. "Out of the frying pan."

I covered my nerves with hopeful sarcasm. "At least the fire has pepperoni. And olives."

"Thank God for small favors," he said, and led me by the hand into the house.

Corey was in the kitchen when we stepped inside, standing on the tips of her toes to pull plates from the overhead pine cabinets to the right of the sink. Another set of cabinets occupied the overhead space to the left of the sink. In fact, all of the space underneath the counter was filled with working cabinets and drawers. I'd never seen so much storage. Then again, I'd never lived in any circumstance where I'd had enough kitchen things to need that much. The room had only one tiny window over the sink. It afforded a great view of the garden, though.

The appliances were black and silver. A pine kitchen island with a cooktop took up the space in the center of the room, an oily skillet with the remains of scrambled eggs resting on one burner. A breakfast nook in the northwest corner served as Ben's second desk, judging from the number of books stacked on top. A couple of still-lifes hung on the wall—beautifully painted platters of apples and pears.

Corey settled flat on her feet again with a handful of plain white plates. "Everything all right?" she asked.

"No," I said. "We're gonna have to make it all right."

"Wow," she said. "That's—"

Red finished her sentence. "The truth."

She pulled the plates close to her chest. "Thank you."

"For what?" Red asked.

"Treating us like adults."

I raised a brow. "You're not adults, but you're not children either."

Corey snorted. She started to say something, but closed her mouth and listened instead. "It's too quiet out there."

I honed in on the lack of sound as well. Either everyone had stepped out the front door or there was a problem. Given the day so far, I'd bet my life on a problem. I ran through the kitchen and down the hall, skidding to a stop in front of the living room, where the rest of the kids had the pizza delivery guy surrounded. Faith stood as close as she could get, her face and her halo infused with anger. Ben and Jess flanked her, ready to knock the guy down if necessary. Three-to-one, if a fight went down—and that was before I entered the space, with Red and Corey right behind me. So why didn't the odds feel in our favor?

The kids had backed him into the corner closest to the front door, the only thing between him and them a worn, brown leather chair and a dark green, spiky mother-in-law's tongue in a green ceramic pot. The guy gripped the top of the chair, but not hard, not like some dude in his early twenties who'd expected to hand off bread and cheese in exchange for dollars but got more than he bargained for. He wore a white shirt with Spanelli's embroidered in black thread in the top right corner, and a black nametag that said Dave pinned on the left. Red spots that appeared to be marinara-related stained the hem. The mist had turned his white hair into a mass of frizz.

He seemed far too relaxed. He should be yelling and trying to fight his way out of the room, but he had a smile on his face that didn't reach his vacant, pale eyes. He should be freaking about the red thermal bag he'd set on the coffee table, the one with the hot pizzas inside that he should have already delivered and been paid for, because surely he had at least one more stop after us and he couldn't be late and expect to keep his job.

Wait.

Pale guy with pale eyes and white hair. This was the guy who'd come by Ben's house this morning and talked with Faith about having known me from back in the day, the guy who Addie had assured me wasn't a Watcher.

His halo was a normal, rosy gold. Nothing to be concerned about. Nothing magical at all. But at the same time, there was nothing normal about him. He had a kind of magnetism that had *magic* written all over it. And he emanated a chill over and above what the weather had wrought. I could feel it flowing off of him in waves from where I stood in the doorway, ten feet away.

What kind of person gave off both normal and magical vibes at the same time?

I cleared my throat to get the kids' attention. "Back away from him."

Faith shook her head. "Not until I get some answers."

"You say you want them," the white-haired guy said. "Do you really?"

"Faith," I said. "Please."

She scowled at the guy, but she backpedaled a couple of steps. Ben and Jess did the same.

I pushed forward, weaving between them, and placed myself in front of them, arms outstretched at my sides, forcing the kids to retreat a little more.

"What's wrong?" Faith asked.

"Everything," Red said from behind us.

"That who I think it is?" I asked.

"Yep," Red said.

"Who?" Faith asked.

A regular, normal guy who apparently delivered pizzas for a living, a man with a regular, normal halo who someone had become imbued with magic and presence that didn't belong to him. A man possessed.

"That's the Angel you summoned," I said.

The hawthorn out front hadn't stopped him from coming in the door. Maybe it didn't see him possessing the poor delivery guy. Or maybe the Angel of Death was too powerful for most protections to work against him.

Faith cursed under her breath. "Oh, shit."

"You knew I'd come," the Angel of Death said. Not to Faith or to any of the others, but to me.

"*La Muerte.* I hoped we'd have more time." We should've had several more hours.

"Foolish," the Angel said.

Of course. "You were already here. You'd already taken control of the body you're in. You came here this morning."

"Reconnaissance," the Angel said. "It's important to understand one's enemies."

"Is that what we are?" I asked. "Until this morning, it never occurred to me that you actually existed. If I thought it would make a difference, I'd have run away from you. It didn't occur to me to fight."

The Angel shrugged. "That's the difference between what you were then and what you will become, if I allow it."

"And what's that?"

"If I have anything to say about it, nothing at all."

The Angel of Death's—Dave's—eyes darkened to black, his pupils lengthening and widening to fill the whole eye. All black, no whites. Then in the space of a lightning flash, a force flew from the Angel's eyes towards me. It hit me like a freight train. Stole my ability to move. To speak or see or hear.

My legs refused to hold me. I fell to my knees, keeling over on my side. My head hit the floor hard. I tried to draw breath, but couldn't seem to get air into my lungs. They ached for the lack. The aching ratcheted to throbbing, then to screaming.

Consciousness fled in a flurry of black-feathered wings. The Angel's wings.

CHAPTER 7

A BELL TOLLED once, a deep, bone-rattling ring that made me think of a death knell. Yes, that was what it was. It might've rung out in the world, or inside my head. I couldn't tell.

I couldn't breathe. I couldn't move a muscle. My body had begun to shut down, and my brain would follow accordingly any second. Darkness filled my eyes, and the sound of wings filled my ears. The only part of me that could act—the only part of me that could fight whatever the Angel of Death had done to me—was my will and the extension of my will—my magic.

I sent my magic forth, sliding into mind after mind, seeing and feeling through their eyes and their senses.

I saw myself through Faith's eyes, lying on the hardwood floor in Ben's living room, unconscious and unresponsive. She screamed, her mouth trembling as the sound rolled out of her. She said my name over and over again. And she shook me, shook me hard, willing me to open my eyes.

My magic seeped into Corey, who held Faith by the shoulders, leveraging all of her body weight to pull Faith off of me. She couldn't do it—not until Jess piled on and two against one shifted the odds. Faith fought them, squirming, flailing to get free. Jess applied more pressure. All of her weight. All of her will. An ounce of Watcher magic—increased strength. When she thought she had things in hand, she glanced over her shoulder at Ben, who stood between the Angel of Death and the rest of us, his feet planted wide, arms stretched to full length at his sides. His gray halo had taken on the form of bricks, a full wall of them. He was shielding us—all of us—from whatever the Angel might do.

It was too late for that. Too late for me.

As I watched, the darkness drained from Dave the Pizza Guy's eyes and Dave went boneless, smacking against the wall behind him and sliding to the floor. The Angel of Death had released his hold on Dave.

Red filled the space where Faith had been, his hands moving to check my vitals. His expression hardened when he found no pulse. He climbed over my body and knelt at my side, positioning his hands to start CPR, when he heard Dave hit the floor.

Red knew what that meant. He knew that trying to kick-start my heart wouldn't work, that his magic, which had no offensive component, couldn't help either. There wasn't a damned thing he could do except to look into me, to witness what was happening, and to pray that I could beat it back.

He'd lost me once, all those years ago. He wouldn't be able to handle losing me again.

I felt the same about him. In this moment, I felt it so strongly, it hurt.

The Angel of Death couldn't walk in this world without a human host. He had to possess a human being before he could act in this plane. Dave had served for a time—for recon, for sizing up the enemy to determine whether any of the powers in play had the right magic and enough juice behind it to prevent him from taking a more permanent host. The question was: Was it me?

He didn't know. He was testing the waters. I wasn't the only one with the right qualifications. Faith, for instance, fit them, too.

I knew those things because the Angel of Death knew those things. He'd taken control of my body. He was trying to take control of my spirit, of my soul, of my magic. Once he did, I would cease to exist. I'd be no one and nothing but an empty vessel for the Angel to occupy and use.

I gathered my magic. I couldn't shield myself with it. My magic had always been a weapon to use against others. I knew how to wield it. He would not have me. He damned sure wouldn't have Faith.

The Angel hit me like a battering ram, over and over again, dismantling my will to keep him out a little more with each blow. But each time the Angel made contact, I saw more clearly into his mind. Motives and plans and machinations, all.

The Angel had known me back in the day—making my acquaintance the night my parents died, following me into the Order, riding on my shoulder with each mission I took, with each kill I made. Watching. Waiting.

A war was coming. The war. The only one that mattered, the one that would decide the fate of all the worlds. The Angel knew every single thing that would happen during the war. He knew it because it was his job to know. All events had been foretold.

But there was a catch. Seventy-two catches, to be more specific.

Each of them was a bright spirit—a human, demon, angel, faery, or god—who could alter the course of events before the war began through the use of their free will.

The Angel could not allow that to happen. It was his mission, along with all the other Horsemen, to make sure everything unfolded according to plan. He would need to influence those on his list to be influenced, kill those on his list to be killed, and maneuver into position those assets that would be needed to assure the defeat of the opposition.

In order to do that, the Angel would need a human body, one with enough inherent magic to be able to contain him. If he could possess the body of someone who could otherwise do him great harm, so much the better.

The Angel had come to Portland not just to find a body of his own, but to kill someone who might dare alter the course of events. Because I could see into the Angel's mind, I could see the face of the one he wanted dead before sundown tonight.

The Angel ceased battering against my will and my magic and tried to slip in sideways. He scoured every shadow, every place where there might be a crack in my armor, searching for a way in.

If he got in—if he took me—I would never get free, and the person he'd come here to kill would die. If anyone tried to stop him, he would end them.

He himself could not be killed. He was unstoppable. He was forever.

The inevitable began to seep in: I was not immortal. I couldn't hold out forever. I'd tire sooner or later, and the Angel would find the way in. Already I could feel the beat of his wings against the skin of my will, of my magic, and where his feathers touched, a voice whispered.

I know you, he said.

He'd become aware of me on a very special night when something had happened that made me vulnerable to him. Something I'd done.

Killed my parents?

The one thing I couldn't remember, the one thing that haunted me. Because I didn't know what had happened, my fear of what I'd done could be used against me. It was the one crack in my armor. The one way in.

Because I knew it, the Angel knew it, too.

He searched anew for that way in. In the time it took my heart to beat, he found it. And the line between who the Angel was and who I was started to blur. My edges softened. My edges—

I was all sharp, steel edges. Red had said so, and he would know. He could see into me. He could divine the shape of my soul.

The Angel pushed at the thought, brushing it away. I pushed back.

He tried again. This time, I sliced at him. The razor edges of my soul—of my will and my magic—cut him. He bled. His blood wasn't red, not like human blood. When the Angel of Death bled, he bled starlight.

The light seeped out of him and kept on coming, flowing slow and steady, with no sign of stopping. And because I could see inside the

Angel's mind, I understood that it wouldn't stop, not without divine intervention.

He fled my body as suddenly as he'd struck. As soon as he departed, without any fight to focus on, my magic gave up the ghost.

Some part of me felt hands on my skin, pushing and pulling, moving me from where I lay on the floor to the sofa. Arms encircled me. They felt strong and solid, and when I breathed in—air, flowing into my lungs, had never tasted so sweet—I breathed in the scents of green grass and dark earth.

Red's voice rumbled in my ear, the words repeated like a mantra. "She's okay. She's okay."

"What happened?" Faith asked. "What did that thing do to her?"

I opened my eyes to half-mast, which was all they would agree to do.

Faith pressed her palms against my cheeks. "Night?"

I nodded, which fell short of speaking, but I thought it might be a few minutes before I could manage to form words of my own.

"Where is it? Where's the Angel?" she asked.

Red answered for me. "Gone. He's not in her anymore, and he's not in any one of you."

"Are you sure?" Faith asked.

"One-hundred percent," he said. "Can you go get Night a glass of water?"

Faith blinked. She took off for the kitchen, Corey dogging her heels.

Red noticed me noticing. "Corey will keep an eye on her."

I took a minute to assess the situation. I lay on the sofa all right, but not flat. Red sat behind me, cradling me in his arms. Ben crouched on the floor near the fireplace, backlit by the flames, head in his hands. His halo wept, full of the feelings he didn't feel he could show. Jess knelt beside him, her hand on his back.

Jess.

I tried to sit up straight, but had no luck. My arms were spaghetti, and probably would be for a little while. Red loosened his hold on me and helped. "Jess," I said. "Call your aunt."

She held my gaze as she pulled the phone from her pocket, not once taking her eyes off of me. Apparently, she had Addie on speed dial.

I rested while Jess relayed the events of the afternoon. She didn't have my perspective, but she had Red's word about what had happened to me. Addie spoke on the other end of the line, and Jess passed on the message. "She's on her way."

I shook my head. "Not by herself. Someone should go with her. She's a target."

"Possession?" she asked.

I shook my head.

Jess's eyes went wide. She spoke into the phone. "Stay inside the house. Better yet, inside a protective circle inside the house. I'll come get you."

Red lifted me up so he could slide off the sofa. "One of us should go with you. Since it can't be Night, it'll be me."

"No," I said. "She should take Ben."

Red tensed. "It goes against my gut."

"Because he's young," I said.

Red nodded. "But I see your point."

"Because he's a shield." Of all of us at the moment, Ben was best suited to protect Jess and Addie.

Ben rubbed his eyes with the heels of his hands and stood up. "I'll drive," he said.

"Let Jess," I said. "In case you need to use your magic. Stay close to her."

Jess headed for the table in the entry where the bowl of keys sat on the table. Ben followed. A few seconds later, they were out the door and in the car, rolling out of the driveway at warp speed, judging by the distressed growl of the engine as Jess gunned it.

Red went to the window, watching them race down the street. "I hope they're careful. Last thing they need is to crack up the car or get pulled over."

I swung my legs off the sofa and tried to sit like a person who hadn't been partially possessed. I mostly succeeded. "Thank you," I said.

"For what?" He turned from the window. "I couldn't do a damned thing to help you."

"You helped me already. You reminded me who I am. I used that to fight him off."

"You're welcome, then. Next question is what to do with Dave, here."

I'd seen and heard his body hit the floor through Ben's senses. "Is he dead?"

"No, but he's unconscious. Who knows whether he'll wake up or if he'll be all there when he does. He doesn't have any magic. That means there's a limit to what I can see when I look at him. And it means he might be…damaged…when he wakes up."

I stood up slowly and carefully. My legs thought about ditching me for a minute, but decided to stick around after all. "I'll look."

"You don't have any gas in the tank, Night."

"I'm what there is, so how much fuel I've got doesn't really matter, does it?"

"Doesn't mean I have to like it," he said.

"Fair enough." I worked my way to the spot where Dave had blacked out. He lay curled in the fetal position behind the leather chair. I lowered myself into the seat. Best to be very close to my intended target, and better not to chance trying to stand through what I was about to do, not in my current state.

"What about the Angel of Death?" Red asked.

I looked at him. "It was close. I got a glimpse of his plans."

"Jess's aunt?" Red asked.

I nodded. "He's looking to kill her outright. Otherwise, he's looking for a body to possess on a permanent basis, and he wanted to try mine on for size."

"This is bad," Red said. "Very bad."

"Could be worse. I don't think I saw everything he had in mind."

Red held my gaze.

"He almost found a way in, Red. There's exactly one crack in my armor. The one thing I can't remember."

Red crossed toward me and hunkered down in front of me. "In that case, I don't understand why he left."

"I hurt him. I don't know how. I don't know enough about him to understand that part. But here's what I do know: he'll be back because he didn't get what he wanted."

Faith interrupted whatever Red would've said. "Are you sure she's okay?"

I glanced at her. She stood at the threshold of the living room with Corey by her side. They had the altar items from upstairs in their hands, but they didn't look like they'd been sneaking away to try something on their own. They'd brought those items down to us with a purpose. More summoning, no doubt.

"You get lost on your way to the kitchen?" Red asked.

"Sorry," Corey said.

"Set that stuff down on the coffee table and get that water for Night," Red said.

They did what he wanted.

I focused the tired threads of my magic on Dave the Pizza Guy and sent a single tendril into his mind. It took a hot minute to find Dave, dreaming that he was sleeping in on a rainy winter morning, snuggled under the covers with his Boston Terrier, Buster. There was a girlfriend in the picture, very cute, with wavy blue hair, so I felt okay not worrying about who would take Buster for his afternoon walk.

A knock sounded on the door. It threw me out of Dave's mind, but I'd seen what I needed to. Dave was in there. He would be fine eventually, and for now our best bet was to put him to bed and let him sleep off his possession hangover.

I shook my head to clear it and looked at Red. "Pretty sure the Angel of Death wouldn't bother knocking."

Most likely, that also meant it wasn't the Order. Not their style. Which narrowed the possibilities considerably.

"Well, it ain't a Girl Scout selling cookies in November," Red said.

I reached out a hand. "Help me up."

He pulled me to my feet. "I should get it," he said. "It could be trouble. Or a next-door neighbor."

"Don't think it's a neighbor."

He followed me to the entry to provided moral support and muscled backup in case I needed it. I opened the door to the scent of amber and vanilla perfume.

Sunday stood on the porch. She wore the same black rain slicker as she had this morning, which felt like a lifetime ago. Her shoulder-length blond curls had gone extra curly in the mist. She narrowed her dark blue eyes as she got a good look at my face.

"What happened?"

"We had a visit from that Angel you're after," I said.

"What? Are you all right?"

"I will be," I said.

Red elbowed me in the side. "You gonna tell me who this is?"

"Someone from that part of my life I didn't get a chance to tell you all about over pizza. Red, this is Sunday. Sunday, Red."

She looked him up and down. "You with her?"

It took Red a second to realize Sunday was asking whether he and I were an item. "I don't know," he said.

"You should be," Sunday said. "Are you going to ask me in or should we have this conversation outside?"

Red and I stepped out of the way. She marched past us into the living room, getting a gander at Dave and a look at Corey and Faith, who'd brought the water and taken a seat on the sofa.

Sunday glanced over her shoulder. "Really, Night? Kids?"

"They come with the territory," I said.

"Because of the gym."

I nodded.

Her face lit up as though she remembered something important. She turned to look at the girls again. "Which one of you is it? Oh, you, with the dark hair."

I froze. I'd convinced myself that because Sunday hadn't said a word about Faith back at the gym, she hadn't known about her. How could I have been so wrong? Because I'd been inundated with magical enemies all day, in a constant state of fight or flight. Because I'd loved Sunday and trusted her with my life at one point, and even if that time was long gone, I still wanted to believe that she wouldn't break my trust.

And now, my former lover, the best killer I'd ever known, stood only a few feet away from the most important person in my life, the girl I'd stolen from the teeth of death, the girl who I loved more than life itself. What would she do? If it came down to brass tacks and blood, could I stop Sunday? Could I stop someone who could blind any one of us just by looking us in the eye? Who could psychically anticipate any move I might make?

Faith's eyes were full of fear, and I realized that must be because I'd forgotten to hide my fear from her. Of all the dangerous beings we'd faced today, this one was the most terrifying to me—and now, to Faith.

"Who's this?" she asked.

"Sunday was my friend," I said.

"That's the bare minimum truth," Sunday said. She unzipped her jacket, revealing her long-sleeved black T-shirt and the black brocade vest she wore over it. The hems of her black jeans had dried stiff. They brushed the tops of her steel-toe black boots. Her halo held a tint of rose red.

Faith rose to her feet. "Why are you looking at me like that?"

"You were so small the last time I saw you," Sunday said. "I sometimes wondered over the years whether Night had kept you or given you away. Now I know."

I stepped into the living room, sidling up to Sunday. "The last time you saw her?"

"The night you took her and ran. I knew something was wrong the night before. You wouldn't answer my questions. You rolled over and went to sleep—or pretended to. I was afraid you were going to bollix the mission parameters and that you'd run, and you did. I saw all that in my mind's eye just like it went down. I just didn't see the girl coming with you in that picture, not until you ducked out of the house with her."

Sunday met my gaze. "I wasn't the only one who knew what you were up to. There were two others sent to check your work."

Either I'd done as I was told with, as Sunday called them, mission parameters, or I'd come out of the mission with a strike against me. I would get only the one strike, the one warning. Second time, I'd be a corpse. For the Order to have a reason to check my work, they'd had to have seen a change in my demeanor reflecting dissatisfaction or disobedience. I'd always thought I'd camouflaged the emptiness I'd begun to feel the final weeks I'd been there, but clearly I hadn't done nearly as well as I'd figured.

The last job—the mission to kill Faith and her family—had been a test, then. My mentor had to have known that there was a chance I wouldn't go through with the job. That was a rabbit hole I couldn't afford to dive into. I would never know what was in anyone else's mind, and I'd done what I needed to do.

I wanted to move this conversation to another room, to leave the kids—Faith—out of this. Any second now, Sunday would say something she couldn't take back.

I glanced at Faith and Corey. "Can you two stay right here for a few minutes? I'd like to talk with Sunday out back."

Faith shook her head.

I tried again. "Please."

"No," Faith said. "This is about me."

I took a deep breath, using the time that took to think of an argument Faith would accept. I came up only one, a long-shot Hail Mary. "Then Sunday can wait, and you and I can go out back and talk, Faith."

"No," Faith said again. "She knows something, and I want to hear it."

Which meant that the good intentions I'd had were all for nothing. This was going to play out and I wouldn't have a shred of control as to how. I'd waited too long for the right moment, and now that moment had passed.

I looked at Sunday, willing her to read my mind, understanding the futility, but that was my magic, not hers. "You saw them come into the house after we left?" I asked.

"I did. Maybe I wouldn't have done something so…drastic…if I'd known they would be there. I only meant to cover your tracks."

"How did you do that?" I asked.

"I torched the house," she said. "There may have been a gas stove involved."

"You blew it up?"

"All of the evidence, including the two assholes the Order sent after you," she said.

Faith stared at Sunday, her mouth open.

"I see now why you didn't want to get involved when I asked you about going after the Angel this morning," Sunday said. "I'm glad you kept her, even if I never pegged you for the motherly type. She looks good."

"Standing right here," Faith said. "Don't talk about me like I'm not."

"Sorry," Sunday said.

I looked back at Red, who met my gaze with eyes that'd gone stormy. "That's what happened to you? You joined some kind of assassin squad?" he asked.

"*Joined* is a harsh word," Sunday said before I could answer. "They found us, not the other way around. They gave us homes when we had none, and people when we had nobody. They trained us and gave us a purpose."

"Killing people," Red said. "You did say you had a lot of experience, Night."

The way he said those words—they hit me like a slap to the face.

I rounded on him. "Until you've walked in my shoes, you have no right to judge."

"I just thought—"

I interrupted him. "You thought what—that I ran away from my dead family and from you, and I magically found a way to support myself by legal means at the age of twelve? That some Good Samaritan took me in? That I had a normal life?"

He backpedaled a step. "No."

"Then what did you think?" I asked.

"I was sixteen, for Chrissakes. I knew the world wasn't exactly a benevolent place, even at that age. So, actually, I didn't think. I hoped."

"Hope is a lie," Sunday said.

Red met her gaze. "I guess you're not here to kill us all or you'd have done it by now?"

She nodded.

"Then you don't need me here right now." He turned on his heel and walked upstairs.

CHAPTER 8

THE THUD OF RED'S footfalls on the steps matched the thud of my heart in my chest. Flames crackled in the hearth. Soot, ash, and sparks rose in a cloud as the log on top of the burning pile fell to the side. The girls sat close together on the sofa, the firelight playing on their faces. Dave the Pizza guy lay in a fetal ball in the corner, beneath the brown leather chair. The pies he'd brought inside remained in the thermal carrier he'd set on the coffee table. As the sound of Red's steps faded, the silence in the room took on electric proportions.

Sunday broke it first. She laid a hand on my arm. "You should go after him."

I shook my head. Red had left Sunday and me alone with Faith and Corey because he hadn't wanted to hear any more about the killer I'd become after I left him. Because my nightmare past hurt his feelings or his sense of ethics. Was I supposed to apologize to him?

"He needs a minute," I said. "So do I."

Looking at Sunday, I wrestled to reconcile my instinctive distrust about what she might do with what she'd actually done. As much as I'd saved Faith, Sunday had saved me—both of us—by giving us the head start we'd needed to run from the Order. At one time, Sunday had been the only person I'd trusted. I'd been afraid to fall back on that trust, but no longer. I laid my confusion on that score to rest.

I couldn't say the same about Corey, who looked more confused than the rest of us put together. Her cheeks had mottled to resemble the bright red of her hair, the rest of her face paler than usual, emphasized by the dark blue of her plaid dress. She fisted her hands in the pleats of the skirt, her blue eyes cartoon-wide. "An assassin?"

"Not the knife- or gun-wielding kind," I said. "Well, I've used them, but they weren't my preferred weapons."

"Magic?" Corey asked.

I nodded.

"Holy shit," she said. "And her, too?"

Meaning Sunday. "Yes."

Corey took in that information, the struggle to make sense of it written all over her face. "That's how you met Faith?"

I took a deep breath. "Yes. How…and why."

Faith turned away, walking toward the fireplace, putting a few more feet of distance between us. She combed her long, dark hair with her fingers over and over again. She spoke so softly, the words came out as a whisper. "Please tell me what that means."

"It means that I was there, at your house, for a job," I said.

She drew her arms close to her chest and hugged herself. "My parents?"

Sunday glanced at me from the corner of her eye. She was trying to telegraph something to me now, as I had tried with her earlier. I couldn't afford to take my eyes off of Faith.

"Not just your parents," I said.

Faith placed a hand over her heart. "Me?"

I started to tell her yes, but that word hurt too much to say. I nodded instead.

"Why?" she asked.

"Because I was ordered to," I said.

Faith shook her head. "That's not an answer."

"Because someone wanted you dead. They hired the Order to do it.

The Order sent me." That still wasn't the answer she wanted—that she needed. "Someone was afraid of your magic."

Corey sucked in a breath. "Oh, God."

"What's her magic?" Sunday asked.

Faith looked at Sunday. "I talk to gods."

Sunday set her hands on her hips. "Jesus."

"Sometimes," Faith said.

"No wonder the Watchers didn't want you around," Sunday said.

I closed my eyes tight enough to see stars, only for a second. Sunday hadn't blown my secret, but she'd blown Addie's—and by extension, Jess's.

"What?" Faith and Corey asked simultaneously.

"Eventually, I figured out who'd hired the Order," Sunday said, "but I never figured out why."

"Well, I didn't know any of it," I said. "Not until this morning, that is."

Faith knelt, legs shaking. "So that's what Jess said this morning was all about."

"She was trying to protect you," I said.

Faith's voice trembled, too. "She said her aunt wanted you dead. I don't understand."

I took a step toward her. "I can explain."

She looked at the floor, avoiding my gaze, and shook her head.

"Then let me," Sunday said. "Night did everything she was supposed to do—everything she was trained to do—until the second she laid eyes on you. Don't think that all that bullshit I said earlier about the Order giving us homes when we didn't have them and taking care of us meant that they did it for free. They did it in exchange for our obedience. They did it so that they could maintain a stable of slaves with the kind of magic their targets had no defense against. And if we screwed up, well, there were always a whole lot more where we came from—throwaways, runaways, children who were abused, children no one loved and no one wanted. Disobedience meant death. There was no leaving, either. No quitting. No saying *I'm done here*. Try to leave, they'd kill you, too. Night was the first one to do that and stay alive. They hunted her—trust me on that. They're still hunting her."

Faith looked up, focusing on Sunday.

"Good," Sunday said. "You're listening. Instead of taking your life, Night took you out of that house, the one where your parents locked you in your room, where they abused you. I don't need to know all the terrible details to know that, not when the evidence of it was right in front of my eyes."

"They didn't deserve to die," Faith said.

Sunday shrugged. "What matters is that Night took you out of there. She kept you alive. She kept you safe. She loves you."

"And you? Where do you fit into all this exactly?" Faith asked. "Night didn't know you were even there because you weren't supposed to be there. You disobeyed, too. Why?"

"Because I loved her," Sunday said. "I still do. And that's why I'm here now."

My raw nerves shot to attention. She'd tried to telegraph something to me earlier. I hadn't been able to hear it. "You didn't come here because you tracked the Angel of Death to the house."

She shook her head. "We're going to have company. One operative, winging his way here on a chartered jet right now."

The Order. "What are his instructions?" I asked.

"To take you both out," she said. "You and Faith."

"But not you?"

"The Order doesn't know I'm here. The only reason they know you're here is because—"

Faith interrupted. "Because of me. Because I used my magic."

Sunday nodded. "There was only so much I could do—taking out the ones the Order sent after you, burning down the house—neither of those things could camouflage the fact that there was a body missing from the rubble. Four adults, but no child. The Order knew she was alive. They've been looking for her the same as they've been looking for you, Night."

"Thanks for doing what you could," I said.

She flashed me a ghost of a grin. "You'd have done the same for me."

She was right.

"We've got to go now," she said.

"Where?"

"Anywhere, Night. We need distance from that operative. A lot of distance."

I rubbed the bridge of my nose.

"Night?"

"No," I said. "There's nowhere to go. It's not just the Order, it's the Angel. He'll be back for me. We run, he'll follow. And if we run, we have him breathing down our necks and an Order operative coming from heaven only knows where."

Sunday nodded. "If we stay, the operative comes here, where we know the lay of the land, the layout of the house. We can take care of him here."

"I'm thinking that's our best shot," I said.

"Agreed." Sunday looked at Corey. "You live here?"

Corey shook her head. "Just Ben. His dad's out of town."

"And where's Ben?" Sunday asked.

I answered. "He and a girl named Jess went to pick up Jess's aunt Addie. Jess and Addie are Watchers."

Sunday stared at me. "Not the same—"

"Yep," I said, and held up a hand to forestall the apology for spilling about the Watchers that was about to roll out of her mouth.

Faith grabbed hold of the sofa arm and pulled herself upright. "Can we have that talk now, Night?"

"Get your jacket," I said.

Faith ducked out of the living room, heading for the coat rack.

I met Sunday's gaze. "I'll be a few minutes."

"Faith's lucky to have you," she said.

"No," I said, "I'm lucky to have her."

Sunday shrugged out of her slicker and tossed it over the arm of the sofa. "I'll take a look around. Size up our situation. You know you're going to have to remember who you used to be if we're going to live through this, right? You can't be the kinder, gentler you with an Order operative. You have to be ruthless."

"Yeah, I know," I said.

"Can you do it?"

"For Faith? Yes."

Sunday stepped in closer. "You know this isn't just about Faith, right?"

"The Order? Yes, it is."

"No," Sunday said. "It's all about the Angel, like I told you earlier. It's about the end of the world. Choosing sides. Fighting."

I didn't know what to do about that, so I didn't know what to say. "I can only worry about one thing right now."

Sunday nodded. "I know what you're going to say, and I'm tempted to agree already, but I have to ask. Shouldn't we get the civilians out of the house? Send them somewhere?"

"They're safer with us," I said.

"Because of the Angel," Sunday said.

"Because most of the people I trust are in this house." And because sending Faith away would only make her a bigger, lonelier target for the Order, and for Addie should she choose to go her own way. "We probably should move Dave."

I caught movement from the corner of my eye. Faith, her jacket on and zipped, waiting for me. We left Sunday with Corey. I debated the wisdom of that all the way to the porch, but finally decided that Sunday could teach Corey a few things, and vice versa.

We stepped outside. The temperature had dropped about ten degrees; the afternoon had moved on while Dave had been rendered unconscious and I'd fought for possession of my own body, while my former lover had come to warn us of an impending attack, Red had decided I was unredeemable, and the girl I thought of as my daughter discovered that I'd killed her parents and been ordered to kill her, too.

The mist had taken a break. The sky was still gray, but the quality of the light had changed, allowing a little more illumination, enough to make the droplets that covered the garden shine like diamonds. The air tasted of the cold night to come, and of woodsmoke from

Ben's chimney and a couple of others nearby. A crow cawed, maybe the one that'd perched in the park earlier, maybe a different one. The sound seemed to open the floodgates for Faith.

"I'm trying to understand," she said. "How it was for you, how you grew up like that and came out the other side looking like a decent human being."

Looking like.

"I can't even imagine what it must've been like," Faith said. "It's, like, alien—the kind of life Sunday said that you led."

Alien.

A nest of wasps seemed to take up residence in my belly, wings fluttering and stingers striking their marks. "I might seem like a different person to you than what you thought."

"God," she said. "You think?"

"I can tell you that I'm not—that I'm the same—but they're just words."

She shook her head. "Do you mean them?"

"Of course I mean them."

"Then they matter," she said. "I don't know if I'm gonna be able to handle what you told me in there. I have one question that I didn't want to ask in front of anyone else, one that I need you to answer if there's any hope at all of my being able to deal."

"Ask it," I said. "I'll answer."

"Even if you don't want to?"

"The truth," I said. "Even if it kills me."

She nodded, folding her arms across her chest. "Why didn't you kill me?"

I sat down in the closest porch chair, the one Red had taken earlier. I'd had a lot of years to consider the question Faith had asked. That choice, to take Faith and run, had been the pivotal moment my entire life revolved around. I looked at the garden, at the world that kept on turning while our disasters played out, where billions of people celebrated their own victories and mourned their own catastrophes.

"There's not just one answer, and it's not simple," I said. "There's the obvious answer: I'd never been asked to kill a child before, and when I came face to face with you, I couldn't do it. There's the moment when I realized that your parents weren't the real targets. But they were witnesses, and they couldn't be allowed to live, which was why the kill order specified they were to die. And I understood that you were the one with the magic, and I wondered who could be so afraid of a little girl that they'd want her wiped from the face of the earth. I couldn't let that happen, because I could see inside your mind and I could tell from your thoughts and feelings and memories that your magic wasn't some kind of evil."

Faith settled cross-legged on the floor in front of me. I realized I'd been looking everywhere but at her, and she wanted—needed—to see my face.

"There's a thing I don't remember," I said. "This thing happened to me when I was only a couple of years older than you were on the night we met. I lived in this little house. It was white, but really old white, like old paper, it hadn't been painted in so long. My dad was a mechanic. He was an old man already when I was twelve, like his work had aged him before his time. My mother was a cook in the kitchen at the old folks' home about a mile away. I thought they loved me. I think they tried to, but they were too afraid of me for love to win. Do you understand what I mean?"

That last—maybe it was the truth, maybe it was a lie. It didn't matter. It only mattered that Faith understood.

She looked at me. Tears filled her eyes, but she blinked them away, refusing to let them fall.

"That's why I didn't kill you," I said.

"They were afraid of your magic?" she asked.

I nodded. "They thought I was sick. Then they thought I was possessed by a demon. They tried to have it taken out of me. It was very bad. And when that didn't work, they installed locks on my door and held me prisoner inside."

"What happened to them?" she asked. "Your parents?"

"Red thinks—he thinks I killed them. I always figured the same thing. But that's the part I don't remember. It's hidden inside my mind, and I've never wanted to find it because I've been as afraid of it as my parents were of me."

She turned that over in her mind. "What does Red have to do with it?"

"He tried to save me like I saved you."

"It didn't work?"

"He tried his best. And then the Order found me."

She thought for a few more minutes, then wiped her eyes with the sleeve of her sweater. "So, what now?"

"I need to find out what happened. I think if I don't, it will eat me up inside. And there's another thing—it's a weakness, not knowing. The Angel of Death wants to possess me, and he can take advantage of that weakness. I might not be able to fight him off."

"I'll help you," she said.

"How?" I asked.

"I can go with you to the memory—you can take me with you, right? That's part of your magic?"

It wasn't the way I usually worked with my power. I invaded the minds of others and warped what I saw there. I didn't allow others into my mind. In my training by the Order, my mentor had delved into my mind, sifting through my fear and desire and love and hate like sifting through so much sand. She'd sculpted my thoughts and feelings, turning me into a slave to her will. She could've made me do anything: kill another, kill myself, or worse—there were much worse things than death, after all.

She'd taught me a lesson, one I'd never forgotten.

I'd never trusted another person enough to override that teaching. If I was going to, though, that person would be Faith.

"I can do that," I said. "Yes."

"Do we have time before the guy from the Order gets here?" she asked.

"I don't think so. I wouldn't chance it, anyway. I'm gonna need my full strength to help Sunday fight him, and I should probably go back inside and help her."

"She said she loved you," Faith said. "Was she your girlfriend?"

I nodded.

"She's kind of scary, you know?"

I reached out and mussed Faith's hair. "I know."

"Were you that scary?"

The question startled me. "What do you think?"

"I think you were," she said.

Strange thing to say. "Are we okay?"

She wiped her eyes again. "I don't know. I don't know that, and I don't know whether I'm okay."

Hearing her say that made my heart hurt. "I want you to understand something," I said. "Nothing that's happened is your fault."

"Really?" She shook her head. "How can you say that when everything that's happened is because of me? It's like I'm wrong just for existing, for just being who I am. If I was never born, my parents would still be alive. Maybe they would've had a different kid, someone who didn't scare them so much. Maybe she would've had a normal childhood, without locks on her door. If I wasn't here, I wouldn't have used my magic and brought the Order on us. Or the Angel."

"You're not wrong. You're special. As far as I know, you're the only living person who can talk to gods and hear them when they talk back."

"The Watchers don't think I'm special. They think I'm dangerous. They missed their shot at killing me. Now what? They think they can take you away and then use me?" she asked.

That was a pretty accurate description of the situation. "They want you on their side when the apocalypse starts. It's gonna be good versus evil, and they want you locked up on the side of good."

"That's what they are?" she asked.

"That's what they think they are." A crucial distinction.

"They want to force me," she said. "Why do they hate me?"

"They don't," I said. "They're afraid you won't do what they want, when they want. They don't trust you."

"Well, fuck them."

"I trust you," I said.

"Do you?" She narrowed her eyes. "You held back the truth all this time."

I sighed. "I was afraid."

"Of me?"

"That you wouldn't understand," I said. "That I wouldn't be able to handle it if you didn't."

She thought about that. "Part of me gets it, and part of me doesn't."

"That's fair," I said.

She balled her hands into fists. "Nobody trusts me. If nobody trusts me, how can I be good?"

The question cracked my heart in two. "You're good not because of anyone else—what anyone else thinks. You're good because that's who you are inside. Listen to your intuition, your instinct, your heart. Trust in that. Trust yourself."

She said nothing.

I stood up and helped her to her feet, squeezing her hands to let her know I loved her.

I'd said what I could, and done what I could. Faith deserved the space to figure things out for herself, even if I didn't like the outcome. Even if I wanted to find a quiet corner to hide in and cry.

There was no time for that. I pushed my roiling emotions down and locked them away. We had a battle to prepare for and the clock was ticking down.

CHAPTER 9

COLD AND DAMP seeped in through the seams of the house in spite of the insulation and the central heat blowing through the vents. I shivered, clutching the sill of the window over Ben's bed, watching for the slightest movement out front through the beads of mist on the glass as the sun went down. Waiting for the operative the Order had sent. Waiting to kill or be killed.

Sunday would be on the first floor, watching the backyard. Faith and Corey stood in the room next to mine, scanning the north side of the house. Red had the south, which he guarded at the window two paces behind me while sitting at Ben's desk.

I'd shoved the neatly made bed away from the wall so I could sit or stand as I liked, and right now, I chose to stand to the left of the window. I kept my eyes on the prize, but I could feel Red's gaze settle on me now and again, and I didn't appreciate feeling as if I had a bull's-eye between my shoulder blades. The ghost of patchouli incense from the kids' ritual made me uneasy, too, although that was because it messed with my sense of smell—specifically, my ability to scent anything or anyone who shouldn't be here.

I tightened my grip on the kitchen knife that served as my non-magical weapon, should I need one. We all had them, except for

Sunday, who'd arrived armed with a nine millimeter. I trusted her with the gun. Anyone else would be at greater risk of panicking and shooting themselves or a friend.

What kind of operative had the Order sent? It would be someone whose magic had a chance to work against mine—to neutralize, to overpower. The Order might not be aware that their man would have to fight Sunday as well. She seemed convinced they didn't know, but I wasn't so sure. One school of thought suggested that I'd betrayed her trust when I'd left, so she'd have gone as far from me as possible when she did the same. The other school could argue just as well that she'd have made a beeline for me, for love or for revenge. No, the Order would've sent someone they believed could take us both, just in case.

I hated waiting like this, and the company was uncomfortable as hell.

Red cleared his throat. "Your friend said the man from the Order would be here within the hour. That was two and a half hours ago," he said.

"The operative would have taken the time to case the area. He'd assume we knew he was coming, so he'd wait longer than we anticipated to throw us off. And he'd come after dark. Less chance of being seen that way. It's what I would do."

"So any minute now?"

"Any minute now." I caught movement at my eleven o'clock, in the branches of a tall maple. Leaves rustled and parted. Black-feathered wings fluttered. They reminded me of the Angel, but they weren't his wings. These belonged to another crow.

"I'm sorry," Red said.

"For what you said or how it came out?" I asked.

"Both."

I didn't dare take my eyes off the front of the house. "Then why'd you say it?"

It took him a couple of minutes to answer—so long I wondered whether he would. "It's like I told you on the porch—you're different than I remember. I'm still attached to the memory of you. I didn't realize how much."

"Blaming me for something I can't do anything about is dirty pool," I said. "I keep telling people that I'm not that little girl anymore. No one wants to believe me, even someone like you, who can see clearly enough to tell the difference."

"Guilty as charged." He sighed. "I've had magic all my life. Like you said, I can see the magic in other folks. Mostly, people don't use it except in little ways, to help the people they love, to help themselves. Mostly, they just go on living their lives. Assassins and angels don't rain down on them. They don't have those kinds of enemies and they don't have to make the kinds of choices you did back then, and still do."

"What's your point?" I asked.

"I thought I lived apart from the normal world because of my magic. I had no idea what *apart* actually meant."

"And?"

"It scares the shit out of me," he said, a raw edge to his voice.

Hearing him say that didn't make me less pissed, but honesty like that deserved to be returned. "Me, too."

"After all this time?" he asked.

"Especially," I said. "I didn't used to have anything to lose."

He was silent a moment, swiveling in the chair. It squeaked under his weight. "That apology isn't enough, is it?"

"No," I said. "I don't know."

No surprise that he had feelings about what had gone down today, about being inducted into a world he had no idea existed. Friends in danger, life in danger, maybe-we'd-all-die-before-the-sun-came-up danger. And for what? To become a pawn in some epic battle between good and evil, or assholes who pretended to be good or evil, but only wanted power?

"I need to know whether you're gonna walk away, or whether you're planning to stick with us," I said.

He didn't hesitate. "I'll stick with you until the end."

"And after that?"

"Will there be an after?" he asked.

"No promises," I said.

"Night?"

"What?"

"I heard every word y'all said after I went upstairs."

"Eavesdropping?" I'd have done the same. "Now you know what happened to me after I left your house, and how I ended up with Faith."

"I'm sorry," he said, in a different tone than he had a few minutes ago.

It rankled. "I don't need your pity."

"That's not what I meant," he said.

"I don't need your approval or your condemnation, either."

He took a deep breath and blew it out. "I'm not judging."

"Then what are you doing?" I asked. "I wish none of it had happened. I wish I'd grown up different. I wish I'd had a chance to become something else. But I didn't, and the only thing that keeps me sane is understanding that what I experienced made me who I am. And because of that, I can help people. I can protect them."

"I wish I could say I understood, but I can't ever really stand in your shoes, can I?" he asked. "But I trust you. I believe in you."

No one had ever said that to me. My breath caught in my throat. "Why?"

"I can see it in you," he said. "Goodness. Strength. Determination. Love."

"Your magic shows you all that?" I asked.

He didn't seem to have heard me. He seemed distracted.

"You listening?" I asked.

"I think there's someone down there," he said. "I just saw something move near the top of the fence, so fast I almost missed it. Whatever—whoever—it was, they disappeared into the shadows on the side of the house."

That sounded right. If we hadn't had so many people watching, we'd never have seen even that much.

I allowed myself to close my eyes then for a moment. I reached out with my magic and found the image of the possible intruder in Red's mind, turning it over from every angle and coming to the same conclusion he had. I sent my magic out further—just enough to touch the minds of Faith and Corey and Sunday. I sent them a mental warning.

I looked at Red and lowered my voice. "Stay upstairs. Keep an eye out for our visitor. Guard the girls and get them out if you need to."

He nodded. "Be careful."

I took the stairs quickly, careful to stay to the inside of the steps, avoiding creaks and groans that would announce my presence. Even before I reached the landing, I knew that the back door was open. A mass of cold air rushed down the hall. The scuff and squeal of shoes on tile traveled with it.

I launched myself toward the kitchen. Sunday had turned off the lights, the better to see an intruder. What light penetrated the window above the sink made it possible to see at all. Sunday and the Order operative were shadows in the dark on the far side of the kitchen island, between it and the sink. He'd grabbed her from behind, his arm around her neck in a chokehold. She elbowed him in the gut once—twice—turning in anticipation of what she knew I would do.

She hadn't heard or seen me coming, but she knew I'd be there.

I came in low, sliding on my knees, my grip strong on the hilt of the knife. I slashed the backs of his calves.

He loosed his hold on Sunday, staggering backwards into the sink. Sunday cried out and went down in a heap, feeling the floor in front of her.

I grappled with why, the reason flashing through my mind at the same time Sunday shouted. "Mirror!"

The Order's man had the power to mirror others' magic back to them. Anything we sent out, he'd send right back. Unless we'd taken the time to build a defense against that. And we hadn't. We'd known he was alone. We'd known how he was traveling and when to expect him. We hadn't known the flavor of his magic.

Sunday had tried to blind him. Now, she couldn't see.

If I tried to slip into his mind, he'd have the keys to mine. He could make me do anything he wanted, including kill at his whim. He could kill me by making me believe I'd died, as I'd done to countless others.

He looked at me, hazel eyes framed with thick, brown lashes. A sable Mohawk crowned his head, huge, round opal studs like eyes in the lobes of his ears. He was short—maybe five-five—stocky, and dressed all in black. He carried no weapon. Why would he need one? His magic would defend him unless he was knocked out, and if he lost consciousness, he was dead anyway.

He flashed me a half-smile. His legs were cut up. His blood slicked the floor. And still he smiled.

I closed my mind to him. Walled off my magic. And pivoted to slash him again.

He kicked me in the chest, stealing my air. I gasped as I hit the tile on my back, the blade flying from my fingers. I skidded into the kitchen island, clocking my head on the pine.

I shook my head to clear it in time to catch a glimpse of Sunday standing upright, her suddenly useless eyes closed. She had some blind-combat training because everyone trained against their own power, but she didn't have real-time experience. She wasn't going to be able to fight him well if she couldn't see him. Maybe, bare minimum, defend herself.

She heard him coming—the quick intake of breath, a displacement of air, a creak of the floor—and rounded on him, landing a solid right hook on the side of his head. He fell to his knees.

How? The same way she'd known where I would be a moment ago. Her intuition was ramped high. She could feel him coming before he struck.

He braced with his left arm, leaning over low—out of the range of her fists. He swept her legs. She went down like a bag of bones.

I scrambled to my feet as he lunged for her, grabbing at her, grappling his way on top of her, hands going for her throat.

I scooped up the nearest weapon to hand—the skillet on the cooktop. I brought it down on the top of his head with everything I had. Struck him with enough force to feel echoes of it through my arms and shoulders.

He blacked out. Crumpled to the ground, blood smeared around him, blood seeping out of him.

He wouldn't be out long. Couple of minutes, max.

Sunday shoved him off of her and pushed to her feet, panting.

"Lucky," she said.

"I don't know why." It didn't feel right.

She reached for my arm, wrapping her fingers around it and holding on tight. "I know what you mean."

"We need to take care of him now," I said.

She nodded.

Footfalls sounded behind us. I whirled, breathing hard, frying pan at the ready. And then lowered it.

Faith was in the front of a line of people running down the hall, Corey on her heels and Red bringing up the rear, yelling for them to come back.

"What about *stay upstairs* did you not understand?" I asked him.

"The part where you asked me to protect the girls," he said.

I raised a brow. "They made a break for it?"

He nodded.

"Take them out of here," I said.

Faith shook her head. "It's over."

"No, it's not."

"He's not dangerous anymore. You don't have to kill him," Faith said.

Because she knew now what I'd been. I might have changed, but I would still do what I had to do, even if it meant taking a life.

"Leaving aside the fact that he'd have killed all of us as easy as breathing, he's hurt Sunday," I said. "His magic took her sight, and she won't be able to see again until he's dead."

Faith shook her head. "No."

"Red," I said, "we need your help."

For a second, I wondered whether he'd agree. But the moment passed, and he walked over to us.

"What do you want me to do?" he asked.

"Help hold him down in case he regains consciousness. And if he does, then knock me out fast."

Red knelt on the operative's left arm and leg, pinning him down.

Sunday took the right. "You don't have to do this, Night. You can just put two rounds in his brainpan. You can cut his throat. There's no risk in that."

I lowered my voice. "Not here."

Not in front of my daughter. Not in front of Corey.

I let my power flow freely, letting it take me over, hearing Red ask Sunday what the hell I was risking, not quite hearing all of her reply to him, but knowing what she'd say: as long as the operative was out cold, I could work on him, but if he came to while I was killing him softly, he'd turn the tables on me in a heartbeat.

I slid into the operative's unconscious mind, bringing a mental blade with me that looked and felt just like the one knocked from my hand when he'd sent me flying across the floor. The stone corridors of his mind were darkened, but he'd left a trail for me to follow—footprints that glowed a phosphorescent gold. I found him in a lonely room at the end of the line, sitting cross-legged on the floor in front of a dimmed mirror. Under normal circumstances, I understood, it reflected magic around it so brightly it would hurt to gaze directly into the glass. No longer.

What's your name? I asked.

He showed me that half-smile again. *Does it matter?*

Not really, I said.

Get it over with.

The words were filled with bravado, but I caught something off in his expression.

Everyone knows your name, he said. *They whisper it when the mentors aren't listening. You are a legend.*

Legends are dead, I said.

But not you, not yet. Not the great Black Rose. You are the best of us.

I couldn't believe what I was hearing.

I hope you live a long life, he said.

Some kind of quake had shaken the bedrock of the Order and cracked it open for him to say that.

One last request, he said. *Make it quick.*

I stepped behind him and sliced through his jugular, pulling away as the blood spurted. In his mind, in his heart of hearts, he bled out, the stone room fading around us.

I pulled back into my body, back into the kitchen with Red kneeling on my left and Sunday on my right. Back to the sound of Sunday's sharp intake of breath, her pleasure and gratitude as her sight returned.

And behind me, a different sound, as Faith cried.

I could feel my body shake—it felt like someone else's body for a second, and then I took control, battening down against the wave of anguish that threatened to crash over me at the sound of Faith's sobs.

Corey spoke, her voice just above a whisper. "He's not the only one the Order sent."

I turned to look at her, my gaze raking Faith's tear-stained face and settling on Corey's bold features, her skin corpse-pale and her hair bloodred.

"I can see him," Corey said. "He's standing behind you, Sunday, and he's talking to me."

Sunday growled. "Why didn't he talk to you, Night? You were in his mind."

"He did," I said. "He called me a legend. He wished me well."

Sunday stared. "What the fuck?"

"He didn't tell me anything about another operative," I said.

"Because he was spelled," Corey said. "The people who sent him bound him to secrecy, just like they bound him to follow his orders to the letter, because they suspected him of sympathizing with you."

When I'd been a part of the Order, we'd heard stories about others who'd tried to escape, how they'd failed—or how they'd succeeded, but only for a matter of hours or, at most, days. We'd considered those people fools and traitors. If that line of thinking had been self-serving, who could blame us? All we knew was that without the Order, we'd be dead.

The mentors—the ones assigned to us, and the mysterious ones we heard about but never saw—they kept us safe. They gave us purpose. They didn't need to indoctrinate us to earn our loyalty. If they punished us, it was because we were unworthy. We deserved it, and we accepted our fates.

What had changed to shift that one fundamental thing about those who belonged to the Order?

The one who'd come to kill me had been the same as me. He'd felt something like I had on the night when I'd disobeyed orders, taken Faith, and run. The Order had bound him in ways that were never considered necessary before. They'd stolen the one thing that had kept all of us in line before: honor, trust, the tattered remnants of free will.

"He's free from that binding now," Corey said. "He says the other guy that's here was sent after your known associates."

"Most of my known associates are in this room," I said.

Corey bit her lip. "Not all of them."

Ben and Jess and Addie.

I curled my hands into fists. "Does the other operative have them?"

"He should by now," Corey said.

My nails dug into my palms. "Where?"

"Home," she said.

She blinked several times, shaking her head, pressing her hands to her forehead.

"What's that mean?" I asked. "Faith's and my apartment?"

"No," she said. "The place you feel most at home. Where feels like that to you?"

I swallowed hard. I looked at Faith, who'd dried her tears, wishing I could make things different, understanding that she couldn't unknow what she'd learned and seen and heard.

I turned to meet Red's gaze.

"The gym," he said.

The gym.

"Are they alive?" he asked.

"They should be," I said. "Until the operative has what he wants."

"You and Faith." Red pushed too his feet.

I nodded.

"What are you gonna do?" he asked.

"Get the others out alive," I said. "Trade myself for them."

"Absolutely not," Sunday said. "I make a much better trade."

I looked at her.

"I don't have a kid to worry about, for one," she said.

Something went thump-bump over our heads. Upstairs. In the approximate location of Ben's closet.

Dave the Pizza Guy, waking up from his Angel of Death nightmare.

Sunday gathered her hair and knotted it into a bun on the top of her head. "I'll check on the not-so-Sleeping Beauty. You strategize."

She marched from the kitchen, trailing blood across the tile and into the hall.

"Ben's dad is going to be so pissed," Corey said.

I sighed. "I'll pay for the cleaning."

"Really?" Corey asked. "When? He'll be home tonight."

"That's too bad," I said.

Faith looked from me to Corey and back again. "Can we stop talking about the blood on the floor? I don't give a crap about the blood or the—the body. How are we gonna help our friends?"

All eyes focused on me.

It'd be great to think we could go in stealthy and steal our people, but the second operative would've set up defenses against that. Two former Order operatives wouldn't be enough to get around them. That meant going in straight-up, without any advantage of surprise.

I wouldn't take the girls into that. In that scenario, any safety they'd gain by sticking close to me evaporated in an instant.

"Red," I said, "can you take the girls?"

He nodded. "Where?"

"Out of the city," I said. "Get on a plane. Go anywhere. Just make sure it's far away."

Faith shook her head. "That's not gonna happen."

I put on my best hopeful face. "I'll be right behind you. We'll get the others and then we'll follow."

"No," she said.

"It's the only plan that makes any sense, Faith. Sunday and I will go in. We can handle it."

And if we couldn't, Red and Faith and Corey's presence there would make no difference at all. Steadfastness and half-trained magic would count for nothing against an operative of the Order—and against the Angel of Death. I hadn't forgotten him.

"Sunday was blind ten minutes ago," Faith said.

"She's not now," I said.

Faith pleaded with her eyes. "But she's not invincible, Night."

And neither was I.

Red touched my shoulder. "Sunday's been gone upstairs a long time."

I looked at him, my heart sinking, knowing already what Sunday had done. I ran down the hall and up the stairs anyway, with Red and the girls hot on my heels. They searched all the rooms along the way, and the upstairs bathroom.

I burst into Ben's bedroom. It looked the same as Red and I had left it, except that the closet door was open, half of the clothes that had been hung on the racks pulled into a tangle on the floor. Also on the floor? A collection of occult books that appeared to have been dragged off the top shelf inside the closet. Big, thick doorstoppers with hundreds of pages on spells, herbs, ethics.

The falling books had made the racket that reminded us about Dave, who sat on the neatly made bed, head in his hands. His white uniform shirt looked as if he'd slept in it because he had. His white hair stuck up at a funny angle on account of an unruly cowlick. His halo looked one-hundred-percent human and one-hundred-percent normal, in a rosy shade of gold.

He glanced up, pale eyes brightening when he saw me. "She said you'd come."

Sunday. I'll bet she had. "She say anything else?"

"Not to worry. She's taking care of it, whatever it is."

She was going to get herself killed. "Damn it."

He held up both hands. "Look, she said you'd be mad, but if you could just tell me what the heck happened to me, I'd really appreciate it. Like, why was I in a closet?"

I started to say *to keep you safe*, but safety was an illusion, and hiding only worked for so long.

"You wouldn't believe me if I did tell you," I said. "Your truck's outside. Drive yourself to the hospital and get checked out."

"For what?"

What parts would most likely be injured by an angelic possession? I gave it my best guess. "A concussion."

"I got hit on the head?"

"You fell and hit your head," I said. "Don't forget to call your girlfriend."

He nodded as Corey walked into the room. "Who're you?"

She ignored him. "Night, Faith's gone."

I rounded on her. "What?"

"She was looking for Sunday the same as the rest of us, but then I couldn't find her. The front door's open. And Ben's bike is gone."

It hadn't been when I'd raced up the stairs. I would've noticed.

"Get Dave out of here, Corey. Put him in his truck and come right back into the house."

"Okay," she said, "but you're not leaving me here. And Red's not taking me on any airplane," she said. "My friends are in trouble and I'm not leaving them."

She wouldn't. I could knock her out. Red could hogtie her and throw her in the back of his truck. She'd still find a way to get loose. I read it in her eyes. I understood how she felt.

She'd do whatever it took to save the ones she loved, even if she had to kill.

Even if she had to sacrifice herself.

CHAPTER 10

STREET TRAFFIC HAD THINNED, the splash of tires on the wet pavement coming fewer and farther between now that night blanketed the city. It seemed too quiet, in fact, as if someone or something caused most people to turn away. Mist fell steadily, and wind gusted from the west, swinging the wires from which the traffic lights hung. The windows of the Stump Town Diner were fogged, a tiny handful of patrons hunkered over their dinner. Sometime during the day, the employees had strung red-and-green Christmas lights along the window frame, adding a little cheer to the dark of the year.

Normals going about their everyday lives, oblivious to the danger that lurked all around. I'd never be one of them. Because of my magic. Because of my choices.

We stood on the sidewalk in front of Justice Gym, the chill seeping into our bones, water dripping from the eaves. The gym was pitch-black inside. No lights shone in the windows. No shadows moved. The paper sign that Red had taped to the door crinkled in the damp air. He'd written on it in red ink.

Closed Due To Family Emergency

Any normal person who took in the scene and read that note might wonder what had happened, and if they felt charitable, hope that everything would be all right. None of them would guess that a killer lurked behind the gym door, holding our loved ones hostage. None of them could guess that any minute now, blood would flow and people would die. The only questions were who, and how many?

Faith was behind that door. I couldn't see her, but I could feel her. I shouldn't be able to. My magic didn't work like that. I couldn't wonder why. I couldn't think about why, not while Faith was in there. Not while she was in pain.

All the hair on my body stood at attention, the muscles in my limbs clinging tight to the bones. The fear in my heart grew with every beat, but the fear could be martialed and used. I breathed in the damp and the faded scents of coffee and car exhaust. The knife strapped to my right thigh felt heavy, and it felt right, as if letting go of the trappings of my assassin's life had been a mistake. This was who I was. This was where I belonged.

Red stood at my side, Corey behind him. Neither of them looked as terrified as they should. Their faces—and their halos—showed only determination.

We hadn't said a single word on the drive over. To talk would be to make real all the things that could go wrong. There wasn't much to be said now, either, and so much to be done.

I spoke my few words softly. "Stay behind me on the way in. Let me do the talking. Watch each other's backs."

I pushed open the door.

The familiar perfume of rubber, bleach wipes, and sweat filled my nose and mouth. I reached for the switch, flipping on the lights. The overhead fluorescents buzzed dimly. Whatever magic had kept most of the people away also kept the light from glowing too brightly. Still, it was enough to help me see the interlocked, black rubber mats that covered the concrete floor, the triple-stacked row of black plastic cubbies and lockers that covered the long wall in front of me, and the brown suede sofa on the right.

Ben perched on the edge of the sofa, his wrists zip-tied in front of him, a similar job done on his ankles. His eyes widened when he caught sight of me, and he opened his mouth but no words fell out. He'd been rendered mute.

I reached him in three strides, pulling my knife to slice through his bonds. I intended to whisper, to ask him for a report on the situation around the corner and down the short staircase, on the gym floor. I got no further than the thought. I couldn't make my mouth move.

I felt wary of trying to reach him with my magic. Surely the Order operative knew I'd be coming. He'd have made preparations against my magic. If I used it and ended up trapped or dead because of it, what would happen to Faith? What would happen to all of them?

If I didn't try, and I missed something important, we'd all end up in the ground and that would somehow be worse.

I took hold of Ben's hands and squeezed tightly, bending my forehead to touch his. I probed for a way through his considerable defenses—and understood why the Order's man had left Ben out here. Ben was the shield. He could protect his people if he was close enough. Out here, he'd be just far away enough not to do them a damn bit of good. And if I tried to get information out of him, I wouldn't be able to do it. Unless he let me in. Which he was magically designed not to do.

He tried. He peeled apart the pieces of his magic far enough for me to catch a brief glimpse of what we faced. The Order's man: five-seven and skin-and-bones, with long, braided black hair and dark brown eyes. Vietnamese descent. He'd done the magical preparation, set the snare that I'd fall into if I so much as breathed harder—or set loose an ounce more magic from my body. The trap would damp my magic. I wouldn't be able to see halos. I wouldn't be able to slip into others' minds. It wouldn't affect me physically, only magically. I would be —normal.

The Order's man had done all of this, but he was no danger to anyone right now. He lay on the floor at Faith's feet, unconscious, his breathing slow and labored. The man was seconds from death. Faith made no move to tie him up, or to set free any of her friends, who were trussed up like Ben had been, and sat in a row to her left. Jess. Addie. And Sunday, who had been blindfolded.

Something was very wrong with that picture.

I pulled away from Ben and met his gaze. He couldn't tell me what any of it meant in words. But his halo wept. Just like it had after he'd tried to shield us all from the Angel of Death but failed, after the Angel had dragged me under and fought to take me over. After I'd wounded the Angel and come back to myself, lucky as hell.

I raised a brow, asking him to confirm the only way I could.

Ben nodded.

I pushed to my feet and pointed at him, pointed to Red and Corey. He got the message.

I turned toward the stairs, taking them two at a time on my way down to the floor, where Faith stood guard over our friends, holding them prisoner. That Faith was not my Faith. She'd been taken over.

Her halo shimmered silver, its usual color and character when she wasn't angry or upset. That and the fact that she showed no fury, no unbridled emotion, would've set me on edge all by itself. The cold that flowed off of her in waves—a chill far more powerful than the cold outside—and the magnetism in her gaze when she glanced at me told me exactly who I was dealing with. The Angel of Death.

He'd taken possession of Faith. She had the kind of magic that the Watchers had been willing to wipe from the face of the earth, and it was deep and wide enough—as young as she was in years and to her power—to sustain the Angel should he choose to make Faith's body his permanent home.

He'd possessed Dave, but not fully. He'd used Dave for a time, gathering information, never intending to stay. Never intending to make Dave his home.

The Angel had never fully possessed me. I'd fought hard, and I'd wounded him, and I'd been aware the whole time of what he was trying to do. Was Faith aware? Was she in there somewhere, still fighting? Had the Angel's presence put her soul to sleep? Or had his taking over, if he intended it to be permanent, killed her soul?

My limited knowledge of and experience with possession aside, who the hell knew the consequences of possession by a being that powerful?

Addie might. She was a Watcher, descended from angels. She'd been gagged by the Order operative's spell, and I couldn't reach far enough with my magic to slip into her mind without triggering the trap the operative had set for me.

I walked slowly towards Faith, splitting my focus between her and the operative, whose chest rose and fell as I watched, and then rose and fell a final time. His death meant the end of the magic he'd used in life. Which meant the magical gag and the trap ought to be history.

I opened my mouth. Nothing came out.

I stared at Faith. A slow grin curved her lips—the Angel's lips. Whatever spells had been cast here, the Order operative hadn't retained ownership of his own spell.

I didn't see or hear or feel the operative's soul leave his body, but I hoped Corey did. I hoped she held him here in this place and asked him every question under the sun. We needed any information the operative could contribute. What the Order had planned. What the operatives planned, if that turned out to be different from what the mentors had in mind. And most of all, most urgently, anything the operative knew about the Angel of Death.

Because whatever had happened before we arrived, the Angel had complete control now. What the Order had started, the Angel would finish.

I met his gaze—Faith's gaze—and held it, knowing that the being in charge behind those eyes was not Faith, but part of me didn't understand or accept that at all. That part of me only saw my daughter imprisoned in her own body, violated by a power that had no care for her other than what he could use.

The Angel looked at me through Faith's eyes. He spoke in her voice, but not aloud. His thoughts bloomed in my mind. *I knew you would come.*

I could not talk back—not out loud. I sent my thoughts instead. *You made sure of it,* I said.

The Angel nodded. *If you fought as hard as you did to save yourself, I knew you would fight harder to save her. I knew you would come.*

And then what? I asked.

I would try to reason with you, he said. *To explain.*

What could you possibly want to explain? Why would anything you said matter? You hurt her.

No, the Angel said. *I saved her.*

I stared at him. At his face—at Faith's face. At her brown eyes and her serious mouth, at the flush in her cheeks, her too-pale skin, and her dark hair, framing it all, the ends curled by the rain. He'd trapped her in her body and taken it over.

Did you take her completely? I asked.

Yes, he said. *I had no choice.*

There's always a choice. Choices are all we have.

You need to know why, he said.

Did I want an explanation? Did I want it more than I wanted to watch his starlight blood flood out of him, pooling on the floor? Did I want it more than I wanted to hear him cry out? I wanted to taste his pain. I wanted to watch as the life drained from him. To send him back to his god or whoever would have what was left of him. Fuck him for what he'd done to my daughter. Fuck him for what he planned to do to us all, for his scheming, for the hell on earth his apocalypse promised.

I'd killed a lot of people in my time with the Order. I'd never actually wanted any of them dead. I'd followed orders. I'd never craved the taste of their suffering the way I did his. If I had a chance in heaven of actually killing him, I'd take it. Even if I had no chance at all.

If I killed him, would I kill Faith, too? He wore her skin. He saw with her eyes. He spoke with her voice. He'd wrapped himself around her soul, if she still had one.

Tell me, I said.

He shook his head. *Show you.*

That meant more than letting him into my mind. It meant letting him into my magic. It meant surrendering control, and all the horror that could flow from that should he choose to turn my magic on my friends. But I knew as well, more than anyone, that seeing through someone else's eyes, walking in their shoes, made those things real in ways that words never could.

There was a secret that I'd never told another soul. It was the one thing that made my magic a living, breathing weapon: in entering the minds of others, in knowing their hearts, they didn't just become vulnerable to me—I became vulnerable to them.

The feelings I felt when I used my magic to enter them became a part of me. When I took lives with my magic—even when I simply slipped behind another's eyes—a part of that person came back with me when I slipped out again. Fear and desire. Bitterness and hate. Regret and sadness. And strongest of all, love.

I did not steal these things. My victims did not give them either. These things simply were, and they became a part of me. Every time I used my magic, the magic changed me.

Red saw someone different than who he remembered when he looked into me because I *was* different. Would he be able to imagine what it was like to carry bits and pieces of my victims with me, knowing not only that I'd killed, but knowing—intimately—who they'd been? How that had transformed a little girl who'd been brought into the arms of the Order with death in her heart into a woman who finally understood what it was to have a heart?

It was wrong as hell and it made no sense at all. There was no justice in it. There was only the growing realization that I'd been granted a second chance and that it would mean nothing if I didn't do something right with it. I'd sold my soul to monsters. The only way out was death. Either I killed myself, or I let the Order do it. There was no other way. That was what my head told me. My heart told me different. It told me not to give up.

The night I'd killed Faith's parents, the night I'd broken down the door to her room and found her hiding under her bed, I'd understood what my second chance was for.

I looked at the Angel of Death. He thought he understood me. He had no idea who he was dealing with.

I closed my eyes. I opened my magic like a blossoming rose, kissed by the sun. I waited.

The Angel entered me.

I'd wounded him back at the house, but I felt no trace of pain in him. He'd been healed by some god or other, maybe even his own.

This time, I didn't fight him. This time, I let him take control. He took me back along the threads of time to an hour ago, when the Order's operative at the gym had been alive and Sunday and Faith stood on the sidewalk outside, drops of mist in their hair, their faces half-hidden in shadow.

The cold air smelled of comfort, of home. That was not my thought or feeling, but the Angel's.

The Angel of Death was the absence of life, after the warmth had fled a body and the blood surrendered to gravity and the flesh began to break down. The Angel of Death was the cold embrace of the grave —the concrete vault, the weight of earth.

The women before him were the opposite. Sunday Sloan, whom he knew well because she served him in all things. She killed with precision and passion, and sometimes with relish. She always would. That had been her nature all her life, and it had come to the fore after she'd run away from her stepmother's house on a sticky July night, fireworks lighting the sky in sprays and waterfalls of color, barbecue and mesquite smoke perfuming the air.

On the street, she could be a victim or she could be a perpetrator.

One taste of her own blood in a rain-soaked, dead-end alley, in the shadow of a dumpster that leaked rancid grease, had shown her that. One glimpse of her battered and bruised face reflected in a puddle, her mouth contorted, every broken-rib breath an agony, made her lash out at the man who'd told her how special she was, taken her in, and turned her out. The man who'd accused her of stealing from him because she'd refused a trick that she'd known—because of her magic, she'd *known*—would kill her.

She met her pimp's gaze and blinded him. She cut his throat with the blade he insisted she carry for her own protection. A few minutes later, she crawled out of the alley. She put herself back together.

When the Order welcomed her into their fold, Sunday had gone with them gladly. Sunday burned hot.

And Faith, who had been raised in a home where the trains ran on time, whose parents had wanted a child they could make into a mirror of themselves, a child over whom they would have absolute control—she burned bright.

Her parents were sorely disappointed in her when they discovered her to be uncontrollable. The more unruly Faith became, the worse the punishments grew. At first there'd been no bruises in places that could be noticed by outsiders, but eventually there were visible bruises and broken bones and trips to different emergency rooms in an attempt to hide the damage done.

Her magic had manifested late. She'd talked to whatever gods would listen, and the gods had worked on the only way that gods did—by granting hope and creating awareness so that when an opportunity presented itself, Faith would see and know it for what it was.

Gods could not act directly in the human world—or any of the worlds. That role was reserved for the beings who lived in them. Angels, demons, faeries, and humans.

The evening I'd walked into Faith's life, Faith had lain in her twin bed, tucked beneath her stained white comforter with the black spiderweb designs, sweating and staring at the ceiling, cradling her head in her hands.

Her stomach roiled with acid. She tasted bean and cheddar tamales and rice in the back of her throat. Her heart thumped in her chest. She could hear the rush of her own blood in her ears.

She wondered whether she was crazy. Who could claim to talk with gods? People who said they did, but no one believed them. And those who some people believed, like saints or the Pope.

She didn't trust what she came to think of as her magic, but she trusted the telltale feeling in her gut—the feeling that seemed to come from someone or something that knew more about the world, and her future, than she did. It said she needed a way out, and soon. She might not be able to find one on her own. During the last year, her parents had installed bars on the windows to which she didn't have the key. They'd placed deadbolts on her door and locked from the outside every night. Ostensibly, the bars and locks were there to keep her safe. In reality, they were there to keep her prisoner.

The room brightened with a lightning flash, illuminating matted, beige carpet, floor-to-ceiling shelves lined with books and boxes of jigsaw puzzles she'd assembled over and over again, and the dry, glass tank where her lone goldfish had swum and chowed down on his fish food once upon a time. She'd hung posters of forests and mountains on her walls: kind of weird. But the images reminded her of places where she'd felt powerful in some previous lifetime: weirder.

A roll of thunder shook the house, glass rattling in the windows. Sheets of rain splattered on the roof, washing the world clean.

She'd known the second Night entered the house. She'd felt it in her gut—the not-right feeling, a change in the air. She held her breath as long as she could, clapping her hand over her mouth when biology finally compelled her to inhale. She listened as events unfolded, knowing in her gut when her mother breathed her last, understanding when her father succumbed a few minutes later. She felt Night climb the stairs and pause outside her door, although she didn't hear a single creak on the stairs.

Faith crawled out of her bed, the sheets sticking to her skin. She scrambled beneath the bedframe, hiding. Not that it would do any good, and not that she needed to hide. Her gut told her that she would live through the next few minutes and for many years to come. Hiding was human nature, and she was human—mostly.

There were places inside of her that felt like...like the gods she talked to. What that meant—what to do about it—was a goddamn mystery. Maybe the woman on the other side of her door held the answers.

The rush of Faith's blood became a roar. The beating of her heart became thunder.

A voice interrupted the vision. Faith's voice. The Angel's words. Tearing me away from the glimpse of what my daughter's life had been like before our paths intersected. If the Angel's vision was right, then Faith had been far more self-possessed than any kid her age, in her circumstances, should've been.

Do you see? the Angel asked.

I shook my head.

She's not what you think she is. She's not human—not all the way. She's part god.

I shook my head again. *That's impossible.*

The Angel reached into my mind, through my magic. He plucked a memory only hours old and turned it over in his fingers like a many-faceted jewel. *Look,* he said.

I did what he asked. I couldn't have turned away if I tried.

I sat in Addie's kitchen at the worn, oak table that was the heart of her home, in my stocking feet. The taste of chiles and chicken and tomatillos permeated the air, steaming bowls of posole *in front of us while we discussed the fate of people we loved and the fate of the world.*

The oak chair felt hard under me. The expression on Addie's face was equally hard. I was a monster. She wanted me dead. Faith was her salvation. She would use Faith to speak directly to her god, to volunteer her services—the Watchers' services—for the coming war.

My voice carried the trauma of the morning—Sunday's arrival, the fear that the Order had tracked down Faith and me, Jess's confession about what Addie was up to, and the memories of the night I'd found Faith that Addie's words had caused me to relive. I heard hope in my voice as well. Hope that I could find a way out of the trap that seemed to be falling into place around me.

"Faith has been using her magic to help with tracking. I haven't yet had a chance to ask her which god she's been talking to," I said.

Addie blanched. "There's only one God."

"No," I said. "There's yours, who would prefer that human beings have no other god before him, and then there's the rest of them. Very powerful ones, worshipped by whole cultures; less powerful ones, worshipped by smaller tribes; and the local gods who walk the earth in human form and set down roots. It's a wide world. You know any of the local gods here, Addie?"

She pressed her lips together until they disappeared, preparing to argue with me. Maybe she saw in my face that arguing would be futile.

"No," she said. "I don't."

"Hear tell of any of them?"

She nodded. "There's the Awakened."

"Sounds like a god," I said.

She snorted. "Supposedly, he—she, it, they, whatever—lurks inside someone in this city like a parasite, waiting for the right time to wake up and take over. The poor person doesn't even know there's something inside them. It's terrible. I couldn't imagine a more terrible thing to happen to a living, breathing human being than to have their agency taken away like that."

"That's all you know about it?"

"I've heard gossip about it only recently—the last few months. The thing is supposed to have infiltrated someone with magic already, so in addition to taking over that person's will, it'll have their magic to boot."

"Why?"

"Why what?" Addie asked.

"Why would a god need a human being like that?"

"Maybe it lost its own body a long time ago. Maybe it can't act here in this plane, this dimension, without a body. I don't know. The only other thing I've heard is that the Awakened is supposed to be showing up now because of the coming war. It's a player."

The memory faded. Only the presence of the Angel in my mind remained.

What are you saying? I asked.

The Awakened is inside of Faith. It lives within her. It's not conscious yet, not yet taken over, but it will. And when it does, Faith will cease to exist.

I sucked in a breath. My legs wanted to give out. I kept them under me by sheer force of will. I wanted to scream at the Angel. To tell him that this was a trick. A lie. He could not use manipulation to convince me it was all right for him to take Faith for himself.

He interrupted that train of thought. *Look again*, he said.

And offered me something utterly unexpected. I had made myself vulnerable to him when I let him into my mind, into my magic. In turn, he made himself vulnerable to me by allowing me a glimpse into his.

The Angel was cold and darkness, a flutter of black-feathered wings on a moonless winter night. He'd folded his wings around Faith's soul, holding it apart from his own, protecting it. I recognized Faith's spirit the way I recognized her halo. It shimmered silver, like stars in the night sky. It pulsed with the rhythm of Faith's heartbeat.

I had a sudden intense and visceral memory of laying on the roof of my house when I was about eight years old, before the worst of the horror began for me, on an April night. The air had been warm but not too thick, and salt-scented because of the southeasterly wind that blew from the Gulf of Mexico. The shingles dug into my back, but I hadn't cared. The sky had captured all of my imagination.

The stars seemed to go on forever. I felt very small. My chest hurt because it was filled with wonder.

That feeling had stayed with me for a long time. I'd held on to it as long as I could.

That was what Faith's soul felt like. Exactly like that. Except for one shining mote in the center of all that dark sky.

It was not a star. It was something alien. Something that had nothing to do with Faith. It pulsed with a beat all its own, not quite aligned with Faith, not quite at odds.

What is that? I asked.

The god inside of her, the Angel said. *It's small now, like you were in your memory, but it will grow.*

A part of me held on to the furious accusations of lies and manipulation with grasping fingers, but the rest couldn't ignore the evidence right in front of me. And the being who had shown it to me, at possible cost to himself, was not the Father of Lies. He was the Angel of Death.

He'd known me for many years, since the night my own parents died. He'd followed me all these years, watching me—watching over me. He knew me. And I knew him.

This was no illusion.

How long does she have? I asked.

It could be years before the Awakened takes her over. It could be never, he said. *It's up to you.*

Meaning that Faith had a time bomb inside of her, and if I allowed —or accepted—the Angel to possess her permanently, the god inside of her might never wake up.

Is it evil? I asked.

The Angel shook his head. *It is what it is.*

Not human. Not bound by human morals or ethics or codes. According to the Watchers, a player in the apocalypse. The Awakened would be an unknown quantity. It would fight on whatever side it saw fit. It could be a boon. Or a disaster. There was no way to know.

The only thing we knew for sure was that it would obliterate Faith.

Is there any chance of fighting it? I asked. *That Faith can fight it?*

There's always a chance, the Angel said.

But no guarantees.

I've saved her, the Angel said.

And maybe he had. But he'd done it by taking away her choice. By taking away her life.

The Angel was not a neutral party in the coming war. He had a job to do. He had orders. Missions that involved killing, lining up the pieces on the chessboard so that things would play out the way his boss wanted once the first proverbial shot was fired.

Was taking the Awakened out of play part of the plan? Was eliminating Faith?

The Angel knew me, and I knew him. But I didn't trust him.

The feeling is mutual, he said. *Open your eyes.*

I looked at him—wearing Faith's clothes, Faith's body—and then I glanced over my shoulder at what appeared to be an empty gym. It wasn't empty. I could make out Red's grass green and earth halo and Corey's bone white. I couldn't see them as clearly as usual, but then they were shielded by Ben's stone gray halo. He protected them while they worked on something, and I'd bet a cool million it involved partnering with the ghost of the Order operative and taking down the spell that held us all mute and kept me from being able to use my magic the way I'd been trained to.

I felt Red's eyes on me, the brush of them on my skin raising the fine hairs on the back of my neck. He looked at me, and he saw into me. He knew the situation, and he understood the stakes.

A soul-deep fear seized my heart. This time, I couldn't pry its fingers away. I couldn't shove it behind some locked door in the recesses of my mind and pretend it didn't exist. I could see only one way forward, and it was everything I'd run from when I'd left the Order.

What if the only way to stop the Angel from using Faith for his own ends, however bloody and violent they might be, was to kill her? What if I'd saved her in the first place—hoping to give her the kind of life I'd never had, the kind of life she deserved to have—only to take it away?

Even the thought burned my heart, seared my soul.

Could I do it if I had to? Could I look my girl in the eye and end her?

Surely the Angel would kill me if I did, but what would that matter? If I had to die, so be it. But Faith?

The Angel followed my thoughts and feelings as they bloomed inside me. A line formed in the middle of his forehead—Faith's forehead—as he considered the lengths I might go to.

We have different ideas about what it means to save someone, I said.

He made no reply.

He also made no move to stop Red and the others from unwinding the spells that hindered us. He could've. He was big enough and powerful enough to focus on more than one thing at a time. I ran through the possible reasons why.

Nothing that Red and the kids could do would make a difference to the Angel's immediate plans. He didn't care about anything except making Faith his permanent host, or controlling the Awakened and Faith, or eliminating the Awakened and Faith.

I'd wounded the Angel back at the house. Maybe the wound drained his magic and his ability to act against multiple threats.

Either of those made a certain kind of battlefield sense. I understood them because I'd experienced similar situations. In each case, I could anticipate the Angel's strategy and counter his thinking, his actions. Even if I had no chance at all of coming out on top in the end, I could do a hell of a lot of damage. Go down swinging. Hurt him in ways that he couldn't imagine. And if I got lucky, hurt him permanently.

That brought a slick, determined grin to my face.

The grin faded because those lines of thought, while easy to understand, and the questions they raised, were the wrong ones.

One more possible reason for the Angel's actions emerged, one I didn't understand. The Angel feared me. It feared what I would do. And it wasn't because I'd rather see Faith dead than used as the Angel's host. The Angel worried about me for another reason.

He'd taken notice of me all those years ago. He'd tracked me through my time with the Order, always noting how I'd changed, where I was, what I did. He'd pleaded reconnaissance back at the house—the need to know his enemies, to understand our magic. He'd jumped into my mind, intending to overpower me, and I'd played right into his hands, believing he meant to possess me.

That hadn't been his plan at all. He'd tried in that moment—and failed—to kill me.

How had I hurt him? How had I managed to shove him out of my mind? Those were the right questions. Could I have hurt him worse? How? Those were the important questions.

The pressure in the room shifted. My ears popped, and something unlocked inside of my throat. Whatever Red and Corey and Ben had done, it seemed to have worked.

I tried my out-loud voice. My words came out in full force, echoing against the concrete walls. "I won't let you do this to Faith," I said.

The Angel answered inside of my mind, unwilling to let go of the hold I'd given him. *Nothing I've said, nothing I've shown you, has made a difference.*

I held his gaze, allowing my answer to show clear in my eyes and on my face. My defiance. My rejection.

There's one more thing, he said.

I expected him to tell me. Instead, he overwhelmed me with his presence, overpowering any ability I might've had to fight him.

The Angel took my consciousness, my magic, in his fist and dragged it down into the depths of my memory. He barreled through the pieces of my victims that made up who I had become and shattered them like glass. He dragged me down corridors darkened by years, my shoes scraping against the stone floors, and buried under the rubble-strewn wreckage of the little girl I had been once.

That little girl hid behind a steel door welded to its frame. She hadn't seen the light of day in long, long years.

The Angel battered down the door with his black-feathered wings. He ripped it from its hinges, the metal screaming as it tore. He crushed it in his hands and threw it down, the clang of metal on the stone floor so loud, it shook me to the core.

I tried to run. The Angel held me by the scruff of the neck and refused to let me go.

I tried to turn away. The Angel held my head in place and kept my eyes open by the force of its will.

I stared into the eyes of the one thing I'd never been able to face. My one weakness. The one thing that could destroy me.

CHAPTER 11

THE LITTLE GIRL stood in the doorway, looking at me with wide doe eyes. Her face was ghostly pale, her long, black hair pulled into a painfully tight braid that flowed to her waist. She wore a pink pajama tank splashed with red hearts and little pink shorts. Finger-shaped bruises striped her skinny arms. Her bare feet shrank from the cold stone floor of the dark room where she'd lived all these years. She breathed deep of air that smelled of dust and cobwebs, lifting her arms to balance the two slow steps backward that she took at the sight of me.

She whispered a question. The words reverberated off the stone walls.

Who are you?

I spoke the first words that came to mind. *I used to be you.*

She held my gaze, her eyes narrowing, peering more deeply into mine. *You're not anymore.*

No, I said.

Why are you here? she asked.

I gave her the obvious answer. *The Angel of Death brought me.*

She didn't react the way a small child should. She showed no fear.

No hesitation. But then, she wasn't really a child, no matter how she appeared.

Red had described what he saw when he looked into me, back when he'd been sixteen and I'd been twelve, back when I'd been Rosa, when I'd still possessed the sweetness and innocence that were my birthright as one so young, learning the ways of the world. He'd described, too, the utter emptiness he'd seen in me after my parents had died, on the night he hid me, trying to keep me safe.

I'd had a soul before the events of that night. I had lost it.

The girl who stood in front of me now, the one trapped in the recesses of my mind, was the echo of that soul.

The Angel thinks he can break you by forcing you to face me, the girl said. *By forcing you to remember.*

There was a reason I'd never been able to recall what had happened that night, and the reason was because I agreed with the Angel. I felt terrified that if I knew what had happened, I wouldn't be able to go on living. Forgetting had meant survival. Survival had meant everything.

The Angel had brought me here to destroy me. He'd tried other ways, but they hadn't worked. This way was a sure thing.

So why hadn't he just gone this route in the first place? Why bother trying anything else? Maybe because the sure thing wasn't so sure after all. It was a last resort. A long shot. What happened if it didn't work out the way the Angel planned?

Only one way to find out.

I tilted my head, motioning for the little girl to step aside. She backpedaled, opening the threshold.

I stepped into the room.

The stone floor shifted, becoming the smooth concrete floor of my childhood bedroom, painted with a riot of scuffed red roses. The walls were white, as was the ceiling, though in the dark the ceiling glowed as if it contained all the stars in the night sky. My father had done that as a gift for my sixth birthday. He'd let me help him, even though it meant standing tiptoe on the top rung of a stepladder and reaching as high as I could stretch. He'd stood behind me in paint-splattered, holey jeans, making sure I didn't fall. He'd smelled, as always, of Old Spice.

That same year, my mother had made my favorite birthday cake, white with white frosting, covered with a mountain of shredded coconut. She'd sat me on the tall, black counter stool that she sat on when she cooked and her legs grew tired, braiding pink sweetheart roses from the garden into my hair, scattering wayward petals on her denim dress and on the yellow linoleum of the kitchen floor.

Sweet memories.

But the bedroom itself right now stood empty, and night had swallowed it whole—the top half of the single window looking out on the front lawn showed only darkness, and the air was thick with the rhythmic singing of toads. A window air conditioner, precariously balanced and held in place with rusted bolts, ate up the bottom half of the window, its motor kicking on with a shudder and a whir.

The ceiling light had been turned off, but a single lamp on the nightstand lit the space, throwing shadows in the corners. A low bookcase hugged the wall beneath the sill, my small collection of books—most about horses—huddled inside. My bed crouched in the corner under a white cotton comforter.

Underneath the bed, a small dish containing an egg, the better to rid me of illness—and evil—as I slept. Under my pillow, sprigs of rosemary and lavender tied together with a slip of twine, to protect me and to draw evil from me. Above the bed, a print of Our Lady of Guadalupe, surrounded by golden rays of light, cloaked in starlit robes of blue, lifted by the archangel Gabriel—the better to watch over me, to keep more evil from touching me.

Over the print, my mother had hung a crucifix that I tried not to look at. I think it was meant as a symbol of hope and protection, but I couldn't look at Jesus's face as he hung on the cross, the crown of thorns on his head, and not feel his pain and despair.

The tear-stained pillow called my name.

The exorcism had been yesterday, not that it had done any good. Evil held me in its terrible grasp and refused to let go. By the time the priest had left, he'd rendered me unconscious, heart fluttering in my chest, fever baking me from the inside out.

That had been last night. This morning, I'd awakened to the call of crows outside. I'd huddled in my sweat-soaked sheets and listened, imagining I understood what they said and waiting for breakfast to be brought to me. My door, as had been the case for the last three months, two weeks, and five days, was locked from the outside.

My mother had brought me breakfast. She still wore her nightgown, a long black T-shirt that reached the middle of her thighs. Her wavy, black hair curled from the humidity, and her thick lashes hid her eyes. She didn't look at me. She didn't say a word. She left me a small bamboo tray with a bowl of oatmeal and an orange.

That had been the last I'd seen of her—hours and hours ago—though she'd be along any minute now.

I climbed into the bed, though my grown body was too long and my feet hung over the bottom edge. Easy remedy: curling up on my left side, hugging my knees. I had a good view of the door. I would see her when she came in.

I heard her first, though—her bare feet moving fast on the creaking floorboards in the hall, the key turning in the locks outside my door, the soft squeal of the hinges as she opened the door and closed it behind her.

Words tumbled like heavy stones from her mouth. "Rosa? Are you awake?"

I pretended to be asleep. I forced my breathing to slow. I glanced through my own thick lashes, watching her like prey would a predator.

"There's a man here to see us. To see you. Your father called him. I don't know who he is, but I'm afraid of him."

I didn't want to answer. If I answered, then something bad would happen. Something horrible that I would do. I pressed my lips together.

"I know you can hear me," she said, creeping closer to the bed. "I know I have no right to ask this of you, especially not after yesterday.

And I know it's a sin, because you are what you are, but I'm asking for your help."

I couldn't wrap my head around what my mother said. How could she ask for my help? She was big and I was small. She was grown and I was still a child. She held all the power in her strong hands, and I held none.

She knelt beside my bed, taking my hands in hers. "Please, Rosa. I think if you don't help me, we will all die."

I opened my eyes, gazing into hers, marking the terror in them.

This was no trick. This was no trap. My mother pleaded with me. She meant every word she'd spoken.

I whispered. "Please don't make me do this."

Her head snapped back. "You won't use your power to save my life?"

Part of me wasn't sure why I should, not after everything she and my father had done to me. But the rest? The rest only knew that she was my mother. Even if she didn't love me, I wanted her to.

I slipped out of bed.

She led me by the hand out the door and down the darkened hall, the framed pictures of our family that hung on the walls staring down at us, judging. Low voices floated from the living room—my father's and one other man's. The TV was on, too—I heard a clipped female voice going on in Spanish about an actor who'd gotten married—but the sound didn't hide what my father and the man talked about.

"You take her," my father said. "I'll pay you whatever you want."

The other man sighed. Phlegm bubbled in his throat. "I can't do that."

"But you've done this with others like her."

The man paused.

In the space of his hesitation, I peered around the corner to get a look at him. He sat on the arm of the floral sofa, his legs hiding the orchids printed on the fabric. He faced my direction, but held a laser-like focus on my father, who sat on the scuffed, brown leather ottoman in front of him, elbows on his knees.

My father's halo was brassy gold—normal, like most people's. He wore his grease-stained, light blue mechanic's shirt with his name, Chris, embroidered on the white name patch. His dark hair was buzzed close to his head. A small gold hoop hung in his left ear. I could smell his Old Spice, along with motor oil and chemical cleaner, from where I stood.

The other man's halo was a bruised orange, as if someone had bounced a piece of fruit on the sidewalk over and over again until it turned the color of pain. He had big hands with delicate fingers, which made me think of him as soft at first, but the skin was calloused, like my father's. The corners of his mouth turned down. His eyes looked like beetle carapaces, perched above gaunt cheeks. He was bald, and he wore all black, like the bad guys on TV.

His halo. The bruised orange. It wasn't normal. If the man wasn't normal, then that meant he had magic, like me. I couldn't help staring.

He couldn't help but feel my gaze on him.

The dark hairs on his arms began to rise. He raised his head and looked right at me, pinning me to the spot. "They don't send me to take them away," he said.

I had a half-second to wonder who *they* might be. Then my mother laid a hand on my shoulder and squeezed as hard as she could, not to stop me from doing or saying anything, but from overwhelming fear.

I sucked in a breath.

"What in Christ's name do they send you for?" my father asked.

"To kill," the man said.

"What?" My father pushed to his feet—or tried to.

The man reached out a finger and touched my father's chest. A spark lit the spot. In the time it took my heart to beat, my father dropped like a bag of bones, the fabric of his shirt burned away and a smoking hole where his heart should be.

A wracking sob crawled up my throat.

My mother screamed.

The man launched himself at us. My mother grabbed my hand and dragged me back down the hall, nearly pulling my shoulder from its socket. She yanked open the door to my room and slammed it shut behind us. But she couldn't lock it, because it only locked from the outside.

The man was coming. His footfalls sounded on the creaking floorboards of the hall, strong and steady. We had only one blocked window through which to escape.

My mother kicked at the air conditioner, trying to loosen it from the window so we could get out. The unit groaned, but did not fall. She had no time to try again.

The man opened the door, his bruised halo burning brighter and brighter. He marched toward us, a stink of sulfur coming off of him in waves. My mother shoved me behind her. It was the last thing she did, her last living, breathing human act in the world.

The man touched her the way he'd touched my father, and she fell, dead before she hit the floor.

I wanted to fall beside her. To take her face in my hands and squeeze and shake until she opened her eyes, but she wouldn't. I was twelve years old, and that was old enough to know.

I looked at the man. He froze in his tracks.

I saw a way into him, a path for my magic to take. I slid into his mind and took hold of his power. It was that easy.

Harder was seeing him in the dark, empty, stone room in the recesses of his mind, cold and hungry and clothed only in tatters, his cheekbones more pronounced, his belly distended, that same sulfurous stench flowing off of him.

Anger welled in my heart.

You came to kill me? I asked.

He frowned. *I came to kill all of you.*

Two weary and broken adults, and one broken child. *Why?*

Some children can't be allowed to live, he said.

He'd come to put an end to all of us, but especially me.

Why? I asked.

You're too powerful, he said.

My magic. The evil inside of me.

He seemed to read the thought on my face, or maybe he could tell what I was thinking because I was in his mind, and he could see mine. *It's not evil,* he said. *It just is.*

If it wasn't evil, then why had my parents locked me away? If I wasn't evil, why had the priest tried to exorcise a demon from inside of me? If I wasn't evil, then why had a killer come after me? Why were my parents dead?

Evil is something you do, the man said. *I should know.*

Something you do.

I'd never done anything to hurt anyone, not on purpose. That hadn't mattered. Nothing mattered anymore.

I held the man's gaze. His halo blazed bright.

I told him what to do. I made him turn the fire on himself. I made him burn up from the inside, and as he did, I slipped out of his mind. I left my mother where she lay and walked past the man. Down the hall and through the living room, the TV flashing pictures of yellow police tape and a woman reporter with a microphone.

The man screamed. The sound pierced me to the core. I covered my ears with my hands, turning right, padding through the kitchen, the tile cool on the soles of my feet.

Behind me, I heard the whoosh of fire catching fabric and furniture. I heard the crackle of flames. I felt heat on my back. I hurried out the back door into the thick night air, beads of sweat springing up on my forehead, and stopped cold.

I stared at the blades of grass. I stared at the hackberry trees near the chain-link fence. The gate between the neighbor's house and ours was open. I took a halting step toward it. And another. I breathed in smoke, tasting ashes on the back of my tongue. The ashes of my life as I'd known it. The burning taste of my home. Of the assassin. Of my parents.

A wail filled my belly and surged toward my mouth, but it got stuck in my throat and refused to come out. I choked on it.

I—I blinked. The backyard and the open gate and the sound I'd choked on faded, along with the smell of smoke, burning furniture, and burning flesh and blood and bone.

I stood inside the stone room in my own mind, gazing into the eyes of the ghost of my soul, the soul that had died that night.

I didn't kill them, I said. At the same time, I understood that in a way I had, because of my magic—only I hadn't been responsible for what they'd done, or for what the killer had done. He'd been a member of the Order. There was no mistaking that.

My mentor had never told me.

My soul's ghost spoke softly in the silence. *Are you still broken?* she asked.

I swallowed hard. I had no answer for that. Part of me would always be broken, and I'd avoided that part with all the strength I possessed for so many years. I'd been wrong to do so—not because my brokenness made me weak, but because the things that were broken in me made me who I was. Because of the cracks inside of me—the places where I was vulnerable—I saw the world in a way that a lot of other people didn't. I understood what it meant to be broken, and what it took to be whole.

When my soul died that night, I thought I'd lost it forever. I thought I'd never find it. But here I stood, that soul within my grasp. All I had to do was reach.

I held out my hand.

The ghost of my soul twined her fingers with mine—and vanished. But not into time and space. She'd slipped inside of me.

She was a part of me. A part of my magic, coming home at last.

I turned around and looked at the being who guarded the door behind me, the one who'd hoped beyond hope that I'd become trapped in here: the Angel of Death. He'd pinned me still, forcing me to see what lay behind the most tightly locked door of my memory. I was pinned no longer. He had no hold on me. He had nothing.

He shook his black-feathered wings.

It didn't work, I said. *My fear did not destroy me. Neither did the truth.*

He turned to run.

I reached out for him, too—not in kindness, and not in gladness. I wrapped my fingers around his neck and trapped him the way he'd trapped me.

He struggled in my grip. He was powerful. He was the hand of a god, after all, and I was nobody—just some human with magic who stood in his way.

Except I was more than that. The Order had sent an operative after me, the same way they'd sent one after Faith. Maybe the Watchers had contracted the job, or maybe the job had originated inside the Order itself. I'd bet on door number two, since Addie hadn't breathed a word about a hit on me, and she would be in a position to know. Just as I was in a position to know the nature of the Order.

It was an organization with a single purpose: death. The people at the top of the Order's hierarchy might as well be shadows. I'd never seen a single one in all the time I'd been in the ranks. The mentors trained the recruits, and every single one of the recruits had magic powerful enough to shape them into near-perfect killing machines, operational in a very short time frame.

The people at the top might as well be shadows. Or angels, working under the guidance of a very specific, hand-of-God type. Death himself.

You follow all of that? I asked the Angel.

He'd heard every word, seen every image, felt every feeling as I'd pieced the puzzle together. It was just a guess, but it was a damn good one. I thought he might struggle harder to break my grip on him, but instead he ceased fighting altogether. He only looked at me, his gaze hard.

Who put out the hit on me all those years ago? I asked.

I did, he said.

I'd been too powerful to be allowed to live. When the Order operative sent to kill my family and me had failed to take me out, the Order had scooped me up, made me one of their own. Who knows if they'd tried to kill me again over the years? There were ways to try without alerting the target, after all. I should know.

Having that kind of power meant nothing in and of itself. It was what I chose to do with it that mattered.

The Angel of Death spoke. *You can't keep me here*, he said.

But I could. He knew it, and I knew it. Maybe not forever. I wasn't immortal like he was. And I didn't have millennia of experience on my side.

La Muerte, I said. *Keeping you for now is good enough.*

I set him in the room in which the ghost of my soul had lived and built a new door, crowned with every magic I'd tasted in all my years, from the fire of the operative sent to kill me to the magic spark in each and every one of the people I'd killed for the Order—for the Angel of Death. I wove the spell with everything I'd been, everything I was, and everything I hoped to be.

When I opened my eyes on the world, I opened them to Faith kneeling over me, her hands pressed against my cheeks, squeezing and shaking and whispering frantically for me to open my eyes.

"What did you do?" she asked. "What did you do?"

"Saved you," I said.

She pulled me into her arms and held me so tight, I could feel her heart beating. She was alive and whole and she had a long, hard road ahead. But she had a chance. She had a choice.

A voice—Jess's voice—cut through Faith's and my embrace. The words carried the kind of power and authority that demanded they be heeded.

"It's not over," she said.

Damn right, it wasn't.

I pulled away from Faith in the dim light, bracing a hand on the rubber mat beneath me and pushing myself upright. My legs took a minute to decide whether they'd hold, but in the end I stood on my own two feet in the place that had become my home.

The overhead lights buzzed and flickered brighter, illuminating the stairs that led to the front door and the floor of the gym with the jigsaw puzzle of the mats on the floor, the barbells and plates, the climbing ropes, and the scuffed, concrete walls—all of it. I breathed in the scents of rubber and sweat—and the grass green and earth and tea tree shampoo cologne of Red, whose footsteps I heard approach from behind. His message was clear without words: he had my back.

The whoosh of tires on wet pavement outside and the patter of rain against the windows could be heard in the heart of the gym, and the chill outside seeped in, turning the skin on my arms to gooseflesh.

The world still existed outside these walls. People walked their dogs and rode their bikes and curled up on sofas with the ones they loved. They huddled on the streets and in bars. They lived and they died. I'd do everything in my power to keep them safe.

Inside, the tension was thick enough to cut. Ben and Corey stood at the back of the gym, holding hands, staying out of the line of fire because danger still lurked in our midst. Not danger from the Angel of Death, or from the Awakened—not yet—but from the Watchers.

Addie's silver-framed glasses hung askew on her face. She adjusted them with a wince. Blood flecked her nostrils, though her nose didn't look broken. Chances were, she'd have a shiner come morning. Her Darth Vader holiday sweatshirt was smeared with mud and blood. She shook in her brown boots with barely contained fury. Easy to guess why—none of this had gone the way she'd hoped.

I wasn't dead. Faith wasn't hers to use. She'd been kidnapped from her own home by the Angel of Death, the most important and powerful of her ancestors, zip-tied, and helpless to influence the endgame.

She'd lost control of the situation, if she'd ever really had any to begin with. The Angel had been calling the shots from the beginning. But if she raised a hand or spoke a word out of line, she'd be eternally sorry.

I didn't need to speak the threat out loud. Sunday loomed beside her. Sunday had lost her slicker and the sleeve of her shirt was torn at the elbow, half the buttons on her brocade vest popped off. Her lip was split and still seeping blood. She'd have a new battle scar, but then, Sunday considered those badges of honor.

I looked at Jess. Her chocolate brown sweater-duster brushed the floor, the hem picking up powdered white chalk from the white plastic bucket someone had knocked over in their struggle with the Angel. Her hair had come loose from the knot on the crown of her head, and tumbled in a waterfall of dark curls to her shoulders. She met my gaze with a solemn cast in her brown eyes.

It's not over, she'd said.

Faith took a step forward, placing herself between the Watchers and me. "What do you mean, it's not over?"

"We need something from your mom," Jess said. "We need the Angel of Death."

"What? What about him?" Sunday asked. "Speak sense."

"Night trapped him," Jess said.

Sunday narrowed her eyes, looking from Jess to me. "Where?"

"Inside of me," I said.

Sunday stared. "Trapped. Inside of you. You're holding him prisoner with your magic?"

I nodded.

"Jesus Christ, Night. How?"

"Not now." But later, definitely later.

Faith curled her hands into fists. "You don't get to ask for anything, Jess. I love you. You know that. But your people want her dead. I won't let that happen."

Addie folded her arms across her chest. "You have enough problems of your own, young lady. Don't borrow trouble."

"The Awakened," Faith said. "I know. Whatever that is, we'll deal with it later. Don't change the subject."

Addie opened her mouth to reply, but Sunday interrupted, clearing her throat. "Shut it. I don't want to hear a word from you. Your kid has something to say, she should spit it out."

Jess's cheeks flushed. She waited a long minute to speak, and when she did, it was with a measured tone that reflected more control than her years ought to allow. "My aunt was wrong, even if she can't see it, but that doesn't make it okay to talk to her like that. We're all in this together from here on out, so we'd better get used to disagreeing."

"Long as you understand that *disagreeing* means holding different opinions, not putting out hits on people we're afraid of," Sunday said. "Long as we understand each other, no one gets hurt."

Jess paled a little, but she held her ground. "I can swear that I have no intention of harming either Faith or Night. I make that promise on behalf of all Watchers."

Addie flinched. "You can't do that."

"I just did," Jess said. She didn't so much as glance over her shoulder, but spoke to her aunt without looking at her. "You're bound by that promise. All of us are."

"Why would you do that?" Addie asked.

"Because we need them. I'm not kidding about us all being in this together. Don't you understand? It's the forces of life against the forces of destruction. The ones who are on the side of the people and the ones on the side of fire and death. The games you played before are over. Which side are you on?"

Addie's head rocked back as if she'd been slapped. She breathed in quick and shallow gasps. "How can you ask me that? How can you not already know?"

Jess's face softened a little. She turned her body so she could see her aunt's face, finally. "You have to prove it. Not to me, but to them."

"I've never had to answer to anyone else before," Addie said.

"You do now," Jess said. "I do, too."

Jess was right. What she asked her aunt to do was more than reasonable, and more than Addie deserved, a far cry from revenge or even justice. As long as Addie toed the line, I could live with that.

I meet Jess's gaze. "What do you want from me?"

She studied my face the way she had at the crack of dawn, this time more sure of herself and, it seemed, more sure of me. "The Angel of Death is the one angel we can't see coming. We can't track him. But we know where he is now. I need you to let us mark you so that we don't lose him again."

Sunday set her hands on her hips. "And so you can track Night."

Jess shook her head. "I don't intend to use it against her."

"But it could be, by someone else," Sunday said.

"It's possible," Jess said.

To claim anything otherwise would be a lie.

I trusted Jess, but I didn't trust Addie and I felt the same about the other Watchers in the world, the ones I didn't know yet but surely would meet. I'd have to watch my back, but that was no different than any day since I'd left the Order, and with what I planned to do next, the Watchers were the least of my problems. Besides, it wasn't an unreasonable request, not with what was coming.

"All right," I said.

Jess let go a breath she'd been holding. "Come back to the house with us. We'll do it there."

Red's gravelly voice rose behind me. "No. You do it here and now or not at all. I'll be watching."

Sunday grinned at him. "Keeping 'em honest? I like that."

It turned out the only thing required was for Jess to touch a finger to my heart. I felt a warmth that lingered there, but no other side effects. A look into Red's green eyes told me that the deed had been done properly, without any add-ons or caveats.

As soon as he gave the nod, Jess threw her arms around me. The gesture took me by surprise. But then, Jess had been as up front with me as she could be. She hadn't wanted me to be a monster. She hadn't wanted anyone to get hurt. She smelled of chiles and chicken and tomatillos—of her aunt's cooking—and underneath that, of patchouli incense.

She whispered in my ear, "Thank you."

"See you tomorrow," I said. Just because the world had changed—and we had changed—did not mean that her gym teacher with exceptional intuition would let her slack off.

"It's already tomorrow, and I'm so done," she said. "How about the day after?"

"Just this once." I patted her on the back.

She broke away and headed for the door.

Addie stepped in front of me, so close we stood nose to nose. "I don't understand how you did what you did, but I think I might understand why," she said.

"How's that?" I asked.

"I've made mistakes, though I'm not sure I'd have done anything differently," she said. "But that was then, and now I'm seeing there's more to you than what I thought."

"Does that have anything to do with realizing you'd become a killer's target? How did it feel to suddenly have the shoe on the other foot?"

"Like hell," she said.

"That must hurt to admit," I said.

She shook her head. "You have no idea."

She walked away. I watched her go. She and I needed to have some serious conversations, but they could wait a little while.

Sunday tilted her head to follow Addie's progress up the stairs and around the corner. She kept her attention focused in that direction until the door opened and closed, the chime ringing to announce the Watchers' departure.

"I don't like them," she said.

Who could blame her? "Jess is all right."

"Yeah," she said. "You going to tell me the story of what happened between you and the Angel? I was supposed to kill him, remember? I can't believe you beat me to the punch."

"He's not dead."

"But he's killable?"

"I don't think so," I said.

She pushed again. "Tell me."

I pressed a palm to my brow, brushing my hair away from my face. "Over whiskey. And fried food."

"Like old times," she said.

Not entirely. Looking into her eyes, it was easy to admit how much I'd missed her, and easy to admit how different we were. Too different. But we understood each other in ways that no one else ever would. I let all of that show on my face, and saw the same feelings reflected on hers.

"Who hit you?" I asked.

She glanced at Faith. "Same as hit the Watcher."

"No," Faith said. "Well. Yes. The Angel did it."

Now that the tension had ebbed, I noticed Faith's knuckles were bloody. She'd have bruises, too.

"The Angel has a great left hook," Sunday said. "Sorry I left the house without you, Night. I meant to trade myself to the Order operative in exchange for the others, like I said. Unfortunately, Faith had the same idea. She got possessed before I could say boo, and I couldn't do a damn thing about it."

"Look how that turned out," I said.

She shrugged. "Win some."

If we'd lost? I didn't want to think about it, not with the war still to come. Not in the calm before the storm.

CHAPTER 12

THE CITY AWAKENED in the hour before dawn. The November chill bit through the black fleece of my hoodie, and a wicked wind gusted from the west, spiraling the fine drops of mist in the air. The traffic light at the corner flipped from red to green, the hum of engines and the slick of tires on wet concrete too loud for a woman with a whiskey- and French-fry hangover.

Water dripped from the overhang in front of the gym, splashing onto my head and rolling down the back of my neck. I shivered from the base of my spine to my crown, and couldn't help but grin. I listened and scanned the neighborhood for anything out of the ordinary. The only thing that resembled that description was Sunday, walking over from the Stump Town Diner, juggling three cups of coffee.

She wore my denim jacket buttoned over a plum sweater that hugged her every curve and brought out the dark blue of her eyes. She'd braided her blond hair wet. A riot of curls escaped to frame her face. I breathed in her amber and vanilla perfume.

She handed me a cup, wrapping my fingers around it. "Drink of the gods."

I sipped, steam rising to dampen my lashes. "I couldn't agree more."

"He coming?" she asked.

She meant Red. He'd gone out drinking with us and had gone home to shower and change, same as we had. "Any minute."

Twenty yards to the right, around the corner at the neighborhood stop-n-shop on Burnside, a car door slammed. To our left, the street curved and forked, the parallel-parked cars huddled at the curbs. Out of the dark, the Orange Warrior materialized in his neon-orange rain suit, bike tires splashing through the puddled light of the street lamps.

He caught sight of me and flashed the peace sign and called out. "Hey! TGIF!"

I gave him a thumbs-up. Then he whizzed past, the headlamp on the front of his helmet beaming, the red light on the back of his bike blinking, as always, fast enough to give somebody a seizure. His golden halo lit him up like a sunrise.

"Friend of yours?" Sunday asked.

"A normal," I said. "I see him every day."

Only that wouldn't happen anymore because there was no way I could continue to work at the gym. I'd turned the situation over in my mind a thousand times in the last few hours, and I couldn't come up with a solution that didn't involve the potential for harm to come to a lot of innocent people.

Sunday leaned into me. "Okay if I stick around town?"

I glanced at her from the corner of my eye. "You didn't ask last time."

"I'm not really asking this time. Just trying to be polite. You need me."

I couldn't dispute that, nor was I stupid enough to try. The main topic of conversation last night, once we'd gotten through the Angel of Death story, was the Order. They'd sent two operatives. They'd send more. They'd keep coming until they were satisfied that Faith and Sunday and I were dead. In the past, Faith and I would've run. In terms of immediate self-preservation, running made the most sense. Get out of sight, stay low, hide, stay out of danger.

We'd tried that. It hadn't worked.

They say that the definition of insanity is doing the same thing over and over again and expecting different results, so I figured trying something different was called for.

The operatives the Order sent had been part of the rebellion within the Order. I could confirm that for the one who'd tried to hit us at the house, and Corey could do the same for the one who'd gone up against the Angel of Death—his boss—and come up short. What were the odds that both operatives would fit that bill? What did that mean for the other operatives in the Order's grasp?

I aimed to find out. I aimed to recruit as many of them as I could to fight in the coming war for humanity's survival. For the survival of this world and all the others.

It would be tricky, though, considering the high risk of being murdered, not just for me but for Faith and the others. We'd talked about it, and everyone had agreed they preferred to face what was coming head-on. I didn't think they understood what that meant yet, but they would. It scared the crap out of me, just like the idea of saving the world.

I'd never been that girl—or that woman. But I was now. I'd chosen.

Just as complicated was how to leverage the one advantage I had: the presence of the Angel inside me. He was the magical head of the Order. What would happen if the higher-ups didn't hear from him? What would happen if I so much as spoke to him through the door I'd locked him behind?

There were few people in the world I trusted, few I called family. Sunday was one of those people. If at heart she was the monster I'd turned away from? She hadn't crossed any lines she couldn't come back from, not yet.

"I need you," I said. "You're right."

She sipped her coffee. "Now that we agree on that, I'll leave you to deal with Red."

I raised a brow. "I need to deal with him?"

"He doesn't seem as excited about our plans as we do." She handed me the third coffee, meant for Red.

I took it from her. "He won't back out."

"Didn't say he would," she said. "See you?"

I leaned into her. "Count on it."

She planted a kiss on the top of my head. Then she turned on her heel and walked back toward the diner, slipping past it, vanishing into the dark.

Footfalls sounded to my left—the whisper of sneakers undone by the crunch of fallen leaves. I glanced in Red's direction. He wore jeans that fit him like a glove and a black hoodie over a white tee. His silver hair was messy and wet at the ends, and he smelled of soap and shampoo. He carried a grease-stained, brown paper sack in one hand.

"What's that?" I asked.

"Breakfast," he said.

I raised a brow.

"Tacos," he said. "Egg, sausage, and potato with jalapeños."

"Oh my God," I said. "My hero."

"At your service." He smiled at me, the corners of his mouth curving into his mustache. His southeast Texas drawl was like music to my ears. "One of those for me?"

"You bet." I passed him his cup.

"Where's Faith?" he asked.

"Ben's house."

"I can't believe you let her go." He took a long pull from his cup.

"Neither can I," I said. "I wanted to keep her to myself for a few days. Keep her safe."

"What does that even mean anymore?" he asked.

"Exactly. Also, she's still trying to deal with what happened the night we met. With who I was."

"She needs space," he said.

I nodded. She needed that, and she needed healing. I could imagine how she felt about me, about us. I could also well imagine the affects of being possessed by the Angel. Of understanding that she carried a sleeping god inside of her, one who could stir at any time.

How did anyone handle something like that?

"She's gonna need all the love I can give her," I said.

"Then she'll do fine."

"I hope you're right, Red. I really do."

He looked at me, his eyes filled with kindness. "What about Sunday?" he asked.

"She's around." I had no doubt she'd spend the day finding a place to live, or that she'd stay close.

"I like her," he said. "Against my better judgment. I thought you should know."

I couldn't help but laugh. God, I needed to laugh.

Red took a step back, leaning against the gym window. I followed suit.

I could tell he had something to say. He took his time gathering it together. "You said last night that you thought you should quit," he said.

"I meant it."

"You said it a lot, so I kind of got that." He took another sip. "I don't want you to."

"But—"

He interrupted. "No. We'll think of something."

I met his gaze. "I don't understand why you're arguing with me."

He reached for my hand, twining his fingers with mine. "Because I don't want to lose you."

I shook my head. "You won't."

He seemed to relax a hairsbreadth, but only that much. "We have some things to work out," he said. "A lot of things."

We did. He had a lot of adjusting to do if he planned to spend time with—and fight alongside—someone like me. I had to figure out how to be with anyone, much less someone like him—someone who didn't have the same traumas built into his DNA, who wanted to do right and preferred to do it according to a moral code not instilled in him by an organization of magical assassins.

"You're only saying that because I'm a reformed killer harboring the Angel of Death and the end of the world is coming, aren't you?" I asked.

He cracked the ghost of a smile. "I'm saying it because I have feelings for you, Night. They're tangled with who you used to be, and who we were to each other that one terrible night all those years ago. I want to build something new."

I moved his hand to my waist and let go, stepping closer until I could look into his eyes without so much distance between us. He saw into me so clearly, and not just because of magic.

I brushed my lips against his, tasting coffee and grass green and dark earth. He set down the bag on the sidewalk and lifted his hand to caress the back of my neck, sliding his fingers through my hair, drawing me closer.

Everything had changed; everything balanced on a knife's edge. New threats. New life. New love. I embraced it with my whole being, with all that lived inside of me, with my whole soul. No one could take that away from me.

What I'd been looking for wasn't inside the gym, or with Red, though I fully intended to give him whatever he'd let me give, and receive in turn. The fact that I had a heart to give, and a soul and a purpose that anchored me in this world, was nothing short of a wonder.

What I'd looked for had been inside of me all along. I'd traveled the distance of a lifetime searching for it, believing that it could be found in a place, or in the presence of another person. Not to discount the value of the gym—or especially of Red—but I finally understood that I carried this feeling with me wherever I went.

The place didn't matter. Neither did the time. The one thing I needed to remember most, I held close in my heart. It echoed in my bones. One word, but that word was everything.

Home.

If you enjoyed this book, please consider leaving a review. It doesn't have to be long—even a few words will be very appreciated.

Reviews make it possible for an author to continue writing books in a series. They make a big difference in helping to get the word out about a book or a series. And reviews can make the all difference in the world when a reader wants to take a chance on a new author, but isn't sure whether they will like the book.

Thank you for taking hours out of your busy life to read. I hope this book brought you time to escape into a story, and that it brought you joy.

Turn the page to read Chapter 1 of *Angel Rises*, Book Two in the *Soul Forge* series.

ANGEL RISES - CHAPTER 1

I OPENED MY eyes wide, fisting my hands in the down comforter on my bed. The rush of my own blood roared in my ears, my heart racing. The textured white ceiling above rocked back and forth for an uncanny moment before it stilled.

The warmth of the bed made it clear that the recurring nightmare had released me. I was no longer at the bottom of the churning river, struggling to reach the surface, but home, in the here and now. The ribbed black tank I'd worn to bed hugged my curves. The edge of my panties had ridden up my right cheek during the night.

Dust motes floated in the air, backlit by the morning light that streamed in through the wooden slats of the window blinds. The sage-green walls looked soft and welcoming. On the wall opposite the bed, the burnished bronze frame and mirror glowed. The scent of baked potatoes and barbecue beef—last night's dinner—perfumed the air.

Yep, home.

The sounds inside my head subsided, leaving the patter of December rain on the glass and the deep, steady breathing of my lover, Red.

Breathing deep, but not asleep.

He whispered in my ear, his voice gravelly, with a touch of East Texas. "Another one, Night?"

"Same one," I said. "Third time this week."

He raised up on one elbow and leaned close. His halo—the field of life force around his body—shone grass green and earth brown. He even smelled like grass and earth. Steady. Strong. It was a reflection of his magic, so different from my own.

He studied me with sharp green eyes, their corners crinkled with concern. His white skin still held onto the barest kiss of the summer sun. Shaggy, salt-and-pepper hair framed his face, with a shaggy mustache to match.

His hair had started to turn at the age of sixteen. He'd had a shock to the system. The shock had been me.

He'd lived next door to my family in Houston, and witnessed the aftermath of what happened the night my parents were killed. He'd taken me in—a brown girl splattered with blood and stinking of smoke. He'd hidden me, saved my life, and lost me, all within the course of a single day twenty years ago.

I'd been twelve years old, scared and alone and wounded to the depths of my soul. The Order of the Blood Moon, a secret organization of magical assassins, had plucked me from the street where I lived and taken me in. They'd trained me to use my magic for their ends. I'd become one of them. They were my family. My home.

All that changed the night they'd sent me to kill a family.

No one had left the Order and lived to tell about it—until me. The magical assassins demanded that its operatives obey or die, but I'd broken free, and the Order had been hunting me ever since. I never wanted to place another person in the Order's sights.

Unbelievably, Red had volunteered.

That we'd found each other again couldn't have been an accident—it had to have been fate.

I'd arrived in Portland, Oregon, on the run, with my daughter, Faith, in tow. I'd applied for a job at Justice Gym, which he owned, and he'd given it to me, no questions asked. It wasn't that he'd recognized me—I'd changed too much. But he'd used his magic to read me, and whatever he'd seen had been enough to allow for trust. Afterward, when danger had rained down in the form of the Angel of Death, he offered his help. All the while, too, he'd offered the promise of his love.

I was still trying to figure out what that meant. Opening my heart meant a kind of vulnerability that I'd never been very good at. Loving me also made the person I cared for a target.

"What's the dream?" he asked. "Which test?"

It was always a test. I was always terrified I'd fail, that I'd never be good enough. That I'd never be enough.

I took a deep breath and blew it out slow and steady. That simple act took my nerves down several notches. "Water survival during my early training with the Order. I nearly drowned. Sunday and I made it. Our friend Miguel didn't. We were thirteen."

Red didn't press for more details, for which I felt profoundly grateful. I could still taste muddy water and electric fear, and I didn't want to dive back in. What he did say made me want to pummel him with my pillow.

"What else?" he asked.

"What makes you think there's something else?"

He raised a brow.

"What?" I asked.

"I know you," he said. "Besides, I see it in you."

That was his magic, untainted and untrained. He'd had it from birth, and unlike my gift, it had always belonged to him and him alone.

Red saw into people by gazing into them, marking who and what they were. He could tell good from bad, and truth from lies. He could see the spark of potential—all the possibilities in a person's path. He used his magic to build people up, to convince people of their shine.

And to call them on their bullshit.

"The ghost of my memory," I said. "The one I repressed the night my parents died."

His brow furrowed. "I remember."

"It was a warning," I said. "The ghost said, *He's not what he seems.*"

He narrowed his eyes. "Nothing ominous about that."

I sighed.

The "he" in the warning was the Angel of Death, the one from the Book of Revelations. He'd shown up a month ago, real as—well, death. *La Muerte.* He'd arrived in search of a human body, a vessel, in which to walk the world. He had a job to do, what with kicking off the Apocalypse, and the time had come. I had the juice to carry him.

He'd gone after me with everything he had, intending to subjugate my mind to his will. His plan had backfired spectacularly. I carried him inside my mind now, sleeping and waking—at every moment.

I didn't know how long I could hold him, only that it couldn't be forever. And I sure didn't want to know that the Angel of Death was not what he seemed. Not without a more detailed explanation.

"You feelin' all right?" Red asked.

I met his gaze. "Aside from the nightmare? Yeah."

"No strange sensations? No hallucinations? No signs that the Angel in your mind is breaking free?"

I bit my lip. "You know I'm worried about that."

"That's not what I'm asking," he said.

"I know," I said. "No. No signs that I can tell. Everything feels the same as it has since that night. Like he's locked up tight."

Red mulled that a moment. "You want me to wake you next time?"

"No."

"You sound sure about that."

I felt sure. "If there are messages coming through, then I need to hear them."

"Or memories," he said. "More things floating to the surface."

I'd had only the one repressed memory in my life, not a dozen. I opened my mouth to say so, then closed it. There were plenty of things about my life before the Order that I didn't remember. Things about my parents and the rest of my family. The Order had taken my culture and given me theirs. The missions I'd undertaken had destroyed me further. Who knew what else I might be missing?

My mind was a wonder of magic and power. It was also a goddamn mystery—one I needed to understand.

"Promise you'll let whatever happens in my dreams play out," I said.

"Cross my heart." He leaned closer, holding my gaze.

I poked him in the chest, my fingertip running up against a streak of silver hair and a whole lot of muscle. "How do I know I'm not still dreaming? How do I know you're not a hallucination?"

His lips curved. "You want me to prove I'm real?"

I lifted my head to kiss him. He met me halfway, reaching with his free hand to cradle my head.

I closed my eyes, breathing him in as his lips moved gently over mine, the fall of his hair shading my face from the morning light. For a moment, the brush of his mustache along my lip and the sandpaper roughness of the shadow on his cheeks and the salt taste of him became my whole world. When I looked at him again, the spark in his eyes ignited a fire inside of me.

He saw it before he felt it. I read that on his face, in a flash of wonder that he tucked away almost as soon as it surfaced.

He lowered my head to the pillow again, tracing a finger along the line of my cheek, then down my arm, stopping to trace the lines of my scars. The souvenir from a knife fight, white against my light brown skin. The half-moon below my elbow, darker and much older. I didn't even know how I'd ended up with that one.

"How much time have we got?" he asked.

I didn't need to check the electronics to answer, not with the quality of the light. "Not enough."

He sighed. "I'll get the coffee started."

I nodded.

He planted a kiss between my eyebrows, then rolled out of bed, reaching for the faded jeans he'd tossed onto the floor last night. He stood tall and pulled them on over his beautiful, boxer-clad butt.

I felt a twinge of regret, not being able to appreciate him properly, but duty called. I slid out from under the comforter, the chill in the air turning the skin of my bare arms and legs to gooseflesh. An icy feeling, a flash from the nightmare, settled over me again.

Red glanced over his shoulder at me. He saw what I felt. He didn't say anything. He just made his way out of the room, zipping his jeans along the way. His footfalls echoed across the bamboo floor of the skinny hall that led to the kitchen. From down that way, I heard the door to the freezer open and shut. He'd grabbed the coffee, as promised. Then in the usual succession, the sluice of water from the kitchen faucet filling the kettle. The soft clang of the kettle being set on an electric burner. Sudden heat sizzling stray drops from the kettle's bottom.

Some things, we couldn't do anything about. The nightmares I had. The sense of foreboding. Those things were born from my experiences, my fears. Unless—or until—they manifested, they were only ghosts. If the Angel of Death was responsible for them rising in me? Nothing to do but keep an eye on it.

The one thing we could actually deal with—whatever lay between us—we didn't talk about, as if by unspoken agreement. We spent time together. We slept together. We blew off steam. We played. There was more to it than that, but we tried not to take it deeper. To invest more felt like a greater risk than either of us was prepared to take right now, in the breath before the storm descended.

Our shared history complicated things. Beyond that, my past presented a serious obstacle. It wasn't as if I'd just been a normal person who'd made some bad decisions. I'd been an assassin. There was so much blood on my hands, I could drown in it.

So Red and I engaged with each other as best we could, and if both of us kept defenses up to guard the tender places in our hearts, neither of us intended to breach them. Not yet.

I sighed. Then I pulled on my own jeans and curled my toes in the pile of the champagne carpet. I squared my shoulders and pushed away dread and worry. Holding on to it wouldn't do any good. Better to eat and caffeinate and take a look at it wide awake. Develop a strategy. Make plans. Carry them out. Thought and action versus fear. Fear could not be allowed to win.

That was who I was. What I did.

I padded into the hall, casting a glance to the right, toward the darkened bedroom next door where my daughter usually slept. She'd spent last night with friends—a good thing for her, even if it seemed strange after so long on the run to let her go her own way. Faith was a teenager, and staying over with friends was what teenagers did.

We had as many things to worry about as we did before the Angel showed up on our doorstep. Back then, the Order chased us from one place to the next. Faith and I spent years finding new hideouts, creating new identities, looking over our shoulders. Our vigilance kept us alive.

When we'd arrived in Portland, something shifted. We'd found people we cared about. We'd made a start at a real home. The Angel of Death coming after us changed things, too. We might be able to outrun the Order, but the Angel? How could anyone hide from a being like that? So, we'd agreed to make a stand.

I worried about Faith when she was away from me, but I couldn't keep her by my side twenty-four seven. She and her group of friends all had their fair share of magic, and they had each other. They knew to ask for help if and when they needed it. That was all I could hope for.

The doorbell rang, a huge, startling sound that gonged through the apartment—Faith's way of breaking up whatever shenanigans Red and I might be up to before she used her key. She'd caught us kissing once and had turned several shades of red.

She'd pointed out to me that Red had feelings for me before I'd seen it. She'd seemed cool with it. She'd said as much. But no way did she ever want to accidentally run into us doing something worse—her words, not mine.

I was, for all intents and purposes, still her mother.

She turned her key in the lock and wrapped her hand around the doorknob. No alarm sounded. The only magical people allowed to enter the apartment were those with a standing invitation. The spell laid into the knob would shock any other magic user hard enough to knock them out.

My family and I were here to stay in Portland. That was no excuse to be careless.

The door swung open on creaking hinges, flooding the entry with light, highlighting the thin layer of dust that overlay the small, teakwood table and the hall tree that hung above it, half of its silver hooks and peacock-feather paint job hidden by Red's and my coats and scarves.

The light streamed far enough to illuminate the living room. TV tucked into the corner. A painting of Our Lady of Guadalupe, starry-cloaked and crowned in fiery gold, hung over the white-painted brick of the fireplace. Outdoor snowflake lights, strung across the mouth of the hearth, glowed Christmas colors. A scarred oak coffee table held down a denim-blue rug. Beat-up denim sofa. Scratched and dinged black dining table pushed against the wall closest to me.

Faith took a careful step inside. She met my gaze with soft brown eyes. Her voice had a foggy, stayed-up-half-the-night ring to it. "Y'all decent?"

I rolled my eyes.

She shook her head. "That's my silent line you're stealing, Night."

"Yeah, yeah," I said.

Her halo shimmered its usual deep silver, though this morning its edges tended toward a somber gray. She dropped her backpack on the floor, toed off a pair of black hiking boots that she hadn't bothered to lace in the first place, and unzipped her silver down parka, shrugging it off and hanging it on a free hook on the hall tree above the table.

Her ruby-red V-neck sweater and black jeans looked like they'd gone ten rounds with her friend Corey's white kitty. Faith had managed a shower, and she still smelled like pinion-scented shampoo and soap. The ends of her long, dark, waves were curled and damp. A closer look showed a set of lightweight luggage under her eyes. The corners of her mouth turned down. Not enough to make a frown, mind, but definitely enough to telegraph that she had something she didn't want to tell me.

"Y'all have fun last night?" I asked.

She dropped keys on the entry table. They landed with a musical *clink*. "We did divination."

Fortunetelling. "About what?"

"Everything," she said.

"And?"

"You're gonna need coffee first."

On cue, the kettle on the stove began to whistle. Red lifted it off the heat. He'd heard every word, of course.

"Five minutes," he said. "Or is the world gonna end any earlier?"

Faith cleared her throat. "Morning to you, too, Red."

He chuckled.

Their easy friendship gave me hope. When I looked at them together, I saw a future I wanted for all of us, but it was one I felt afraid to dream. We might make it, but we wouldn't get out from under unscathed.

Where the Order was concerned, no one ever did.

I'd been the Order's number-two assassin for years, sneaking into the homes of targets, invading minds with my magic, using my power to take out the targets I'd been assigned. I'd had a one-hundred-percent follow-through rate on all of my missions, except the last one.

The Order had assigned me a family. Mother, father, kid. I'd murdered the female target in her sleep. Her husband hadn't been so lucky. He'd awakened before I could slip into his mind and take him peacefully, so he got a bullet for his trouble. The child had been the problem.

The child had been Faith.

She'd been like me when I was small. Her parents hadn't understood her gift. They'd hurt her. Locked her away. They'd tried to make her normal and, when they'd failed, they hid her. God only knew what they might've tried next.

I couldn't take her life myself, and I couldn't leave her there for the follow-up team to come along and finish the job. That left only one choice. I slipped away in the night, leaving the Order behind, taking Faith with me.

For the longest time, she hadn't known the circumstances under which I'd "adopted" her. She'd chosen to believe that I'd saved her from the Order operative who'd been sent to kill her. I'd shattered that belief, that innocence, a month ago because I'd had no choice. Now that Faith knew the truth, she'd accepted it as much as she could.

Some days, she blamed me. Other days, she clung to me. I was all she had, and she knew I felt the same.

We needed each other.

I pulled out a chair from the dinette. I pointed at Faith, then at the seat.

She hesitated. "There's a man coming."

"Another Order operative?" I asked.

"Yes," she said.

We'd expected this. The Order had tracked us here. They'd sent assassins after us. We'd taken them out. They'd send more.

"Just the one?" Red asked.

Faith nodded. "It's who he is that's the problem. Him. His magic."

Red sipped his coffee. "The man's magic is the problem? Or he's the problem, himself?"

"Both," Faith said. "It wasn't just the cards that said so. I also got messages while I was reading. You know, from…"

She trailed off.

I'd been in the process of lifting my mug to take the first sip. I lowered it slowly, and couldn't help notice that my hand trembled slightly as I did. I finished her sentence in my silent voice.

The Awakened.

Faith's magic had a source unlike any other I'd ever heard of before—a god that was a part of her soul. No one knew much about this god other than that it was very old and that it slept inside the soul of a human being, passed down through the generations via reincarnation. It would wake from its slumber at some point. No one knew when. What it might do afterwards was a mystery as well—one that even the Angel of Death seemed to fear.

If Faith was receiving messages from the sleeping god while doing a routine divination reading—that meant trouble, any way we sliced it. I wouldn't tell her it was all right, or act as if it was somehow normal or expected. After the business of withholding how she'd come to be with me, I wouldn't lie to her again.

I reached across the table and covered her hand with mine. She seemed to breathe a little deeper. Sit a little easier. I needed to be steady for her. If I was going to freak out, I'd have to do it on the inside.

Red set his cup down on the table and leaned back in his chair, folding his arms across his chest. "Did you read any clues in the cards about what this Order operative wants?"

Faith pulled her hand from beneath mine. "What do they always want?"

Red simply looked at her.

Faith stared right back at him.

Across the room, the front door opened unexpectedly on its noisy hinges. Only one other person had a key to the apartment, not that she'd had to use it this time.

Red cocked his head at Faith. "You don't lock the door behind you now?"

Faith's eyes widened. Red's tone hadn't been angry. He'd been teasing her. Teasing. At a time like this. "Are you made of steel or something?"

Sunday Sloan did what Faith had forgotten to—flip the deadbolt home behind her—and stepped inside the small, stuffed entry. The music of her voice preceded her, like the sound water made as it flowed over rocks. "Never let him fool you, Faith. He's made of feelings. Great big, mushy feelings."

"That's me," Red said. "Pile of mush."

Sunday shrugged out of her black trench coat, hanging it on top of mine. She peeled off a pair of gray wool gloves, tossing them on top of the keys. Thick blond curls brushed her shoulders. She wore the usual makeup on her porcelain face—just a pale pink flush of lipstick—along with a black T-shirt, black jeans, and steel-toe black boots with rubber soles. Practical.

Sunday had been my friend since I'd met her, and more beginning not long after the night of the survival test, when Miguel had drowned in the river. She'd been my lover. My soulmate. My salvation.

When I'd left the Order, I'd left her behind, too. She'd still believed in the Order. She was the best assassin they'd ever trained, and she had a thirst for killing. I wasn't altogether sure that she'd lost that thirst.

That made me wary, even if I understood it. I'd been the same, once upon a time. I'd figured the Order had sent me after targets for a good reason, that they deserved what they got. Simple lies that masked the complex truth—that the Order contracted to kill good people as well as bad.

I tried not to think about my targets—my victims. Recriminations served no purpose. That left me with atonement. How to balance the scales? I had to believe it could be done.

"What's the emergency?" Sunday asked.

I looked at Faith. "You called her?"

Faith flashed me her best dead-on *duh* expression. "All hands on deck."

Red answered Sunday's question. "Order operative on the way. Troublesome magic. Faith's sleeping god thinks it's a problem."

She hesitated on her way to the table, so briefly that anyone who didn't know her well probably wouldn't have picked up on it. "ETA?"

He raised his cup to her. "God only knows."

"Got any whisky to put in that coffee?" Sunday slipped past us, headed for the kitchen to grab another mug.

"Bourbon," Red said. "Cabinet to the left of the sink, bottom shelf."

Sunday returned with a mug, but no alcohol. She poured herself half of what remained in the press, offering the rest to me. When I shook my head, she topped off her portion.

"Changed your mind about the day drinking?" Red asked.

"You understand metaphors, right?" Sunday lifted her cup from the bottom and took a gulp rather than a sip.

"We're screwed?" Red asked.

"Like a porn star," Sunday said.

Faith's jaw dropped, and I stared at Sunday.

"What?" Sunday took another swig of coffee. She glanced at Faith. "Did your god say anything specific?"

Faith closed her mouth. After a moment, she said, "Purple."

"Purple what?" Sunday asked.

"That's it," Faith said. "Just the color."

Sunday leaned back in her chair. "I don't like the sound of that."

"What's it sound like?" Red asked.

"Like a chameleon," she said. "They're the only magicians who have purple halos."

I'd never met a chameleon. I'd only heard about them. Supposedly, their magic could camouflage them under any circumstances, like the creatures they'd been named after. They could also impersonate other people, down to the visible pores on a nose, down to the way a person smelled and tasted. They were uncanny, and the Order only brought them out when need dictated.

Chameleons were great at observation. Infiltration. They were sent in when the target was so important and so dangerous, failure was not an option.

"I was trained in how to spot one, so I should be able to," Sunday said. "Theoretically."

I downed the contents of my cup. "Wait—what? Why'd the Order train you for that, but not me?"

"I was part of a pilot program," she said. "The mentors were testing to see whether it was possible for someone who wasn't a chameleon to spot one—particularly someone who couldn't see magic the way you do, Night. Or you, Red. Soul-blind, they called it. They said it was because the chameleons would be needed on future missions, and the rest of us had to find a way to be able to work with them."

"They *said*?" I asked.

"I got the impression they were lying," Sunday said. "I got the impression they were afraid."

I whistled. If something—someone—had made the higher-ups at the Order nervous enough to show, we should be afraid, too.

"The first and only clue is the halo," she said. "It's purple, and it's not fixed. Also, their souls remain their own at the deepest level. That was what I was told. For the soul-blind, there's a shimmer that you can sometimes catch from the corner of your eye when the chameleon moves."

Red set down his cup. "That's it?"

Sunday nodded.

"Damn," he said.

I sat back. "How successful were you, spotting chameleons for the Order?"

"One out of twenty," she said.

Bad odds. "You get a sense of how many chameleons there are?"

She met my gaze. "They didn't tell me, but if I were guessing, I'd put the number at about a hundred."

"How could there be that many?" Red asked. "I mean, are there a shit ton of assassins who can blind their enemies with a single glance?"

"Just me," Sunday said. "Just like there's only one Night."

"Illustrates my point."

She sighed. "There's a thing that happens—a phenomenon, the mentors would call it—where when there's need in the world for a certain type of magic, it appears. More children who carry that kind of power are born to answer the need. According to the mentor I asked, that started happening with chameleons about twenty, thirty years ago. That's what I know."

"That's all?" Red asked.

"Unfortunately, yes." She looked at Red. "You need to take a look at all of us now, and you can start with me. Don't just look at the way my soul manifests. Don't just check my thoughts and feelings. Look deeper."

"This is practice?" he asked.

"You can think of it that way, sure," she said.

"And we need a baseline check to make sure that everyone in this room is who they say they are," he said.

She nodded.

"You're you," he said.

Faith blinked. "That fast? You already checked her?"

He nodded. It was what he did.

Faith pushed away from the table, rising to pace the length of the room, table to fireplace and back again. The rhythm of her steps grated. The tension in her body seemed too much for one girl to hold.

Sunday narrowed her eyes. "Anxious?"

"Aren't you?" Faith asked.

Sunday turned away without answering. "Night, you'll have to check Red. Can you do that?"

I nodded, then took a deep breath and focused my power on Red—on his grass and earth halo, the way it played on the edges of his skin. The warmth that radiated from him.

I slipped into his mind. My magic melded with his thoughts and emotions as if they were my own.

He trained his whole self—his perceptions and sensations—on me. I saw my face the way he did, through his eyes, noting the fall of my hair along the curve of my neck, the particular shade of brown that suffused my skin, the bow of my mouth. Pressure filled his chest—an overflow of feeling. Some of it was fear for what might happen. Most of it was love.

The depth of the emotion surprised me. I tried not to let that show.

I turned to his memories, rifling through them in search of the one I wanted, filled with darkness, and only a sliver of light creeping in through the crack between the double doors. The light flashed red and blue, red and blue. It came from the trucks outside on the street.

The hardwood floor of the closet hit every pressure point on Red's body. He couldn't lie still, which meant he couldn't sleep. Hell, he was a pure fool, as his mom would say, for even trying. The house next door had burned near to the ground. The fire department's best and brightest had done what they could to save it and the folks inside, but they'd been too late.

The lone survivor of the fire was a secret, and she was in his closet, out like a light and having dreams filled with terror, judging by the way she shook. She reeked of smoke and singed hair and other things he didn't want to imagine but couldn't help—melting plastic and Sheetrock and furniture and…well…people.

She'd wrapped both arms around his yellow Lab, Dorothy, so tight it was a wonder that Dorothy hadn't squirmed away or bitten her, but the dog seemed to know what she needed and had refused to leave her side.

Neither would Red. He'd hide her as long as he needed to.

He mentally ticked through all the stuff he was supposed to do tomorrow. Things he would have to put off. Ride his bike to the library. Catch a game of football with Doug Martin from two blocks over. Work on the book report for his English class on Monday. He was only halfway finished reading *Watership Down*.

I whispered to his little boy self. What did you say to me when you found me tonight? What did you say, exactly?

Nothing, the little boy whispered.

He'd grabbed me around the waist as I sneaked through his backyard, tucking a hand over my mouth as tight as he could without hurting me so that I wouldn't cry out.

What was my name? I asked.

Rosa, he said. The most beautiful name in the world.

Outside the closet, the world was on fire.

A sound so faint I shouldn't have been able to hear it from inside Red's memory raised my hackles. Animal instinct took over.

I let go of Red so fast, my magic rebounded like the business end of a slingshot—rocking me in my chair at the dinette. My vision blurred, my breath ragged. My hand twitched, knocking over my cup.

Instinct took over—I pivoted in my seat and ducked a half second later without knowing why.

It saved my life.

ALSO BY LESLIE CLAIRE WALKER

THE AWAKENED MAGIC SAGA

THE SOUL FORGE

(The Complete Series)

Angel Hunts

Angel Rises

Angel Falls

Angel Strikes

Angel Roars

Angel Burns

THE FAERY CHRONICLES

(The Complete Series)

Faery Novice

Faery Prophet

Faery Sovereign

SHORT STORY COLLECTIONS

Ink & Blood

Ink & Stars

Ink & Sword

ACKNOWLEDGMENTS

This story wouldn't be what it is without Michael Klaas, Miles, Brandon, CJ, Zack, and Claire. Thank you for excellent company and long, action-packed afternoons. To Jo Anne Banker and T. Thorn Coyle, thank you for reading the draft manuscript and for your always-excellent suggestions. And to J.C. Andrijeski, Dayle Dermatis, and Phaedra Weldon, thank you for inspiration, encouragement, and all-around awesomeness.

Y'all make me feel like the luckiest person on the planet.

ABOUT THE AUTHOR

Since the age of seven, Leslie Claire Walker has wanted to be Princess Leia—wise and brave and never afraid of a fight, no matter the odds.

Leslie hails from the concrete and steel canyons and lush bayous of southeast Texas—a long way from Alderaan. Now, she lives in the rain-drenched Pacific Northwest with a cast of spectacular characters, including cats, harps, fantastic pieces of art that may or may not be doorways to other realms, and too many fantasy novels to count.

She is the author of **The Faery Chronicles** and **Soul Forge** series, two complete series of urban fantasy novels, novellas, and stories filled with found family and magic.

Connect with Leslie
leslieclairewalker.com
leslie@leslieclairewalker.com

COPYRIGHT INFORMATION

ANGEL HUNTS

Copyright © 2018 Leslie Claire Walker
Published 2018 by Secret Fire Press
Previously Published as Night Awakens
Copyright © 2016 Leslie Claire Walker
Published 2016 by Secret Fire Press
Cover and Layout Copyright © 2018 by Secret Fire Press
Cover Design by Lou Harper
Cover Art Copyright © Lou Harper

This book is licensed for your personal enjoyment only. All rights reserved. This is a work of fiction. All characters and events portrayed in this book are fictional, and any resemblance to real people or incidents is purely coincidental. This book, or parts thereof, may not be reproduced in any form without permission.

❋ Created with Vellum